By royal decree, Harlequin ~~~~ ~~~~
bring you THE ROYAL HOUSE OF NIROLI. ~~~~
the glamorous, enticing world of the Nirolian Royal
Family. As the king ails he must find an heir...each
month an exciting new installment follows the epic
search for the true Nirolian king. Eight heirs, eight
romances, eight fantastic stories! Favorite author
Penny Jordan starts this fabulous new series with
The Future King's Pregnant Mistress. It's time for
playboy Prince Marco Fierezza to claim his rightful
place—on the throne! But what will the king-in-waiting
do when he discovers his mistress is pregnant?

Plus, Lucy Monroe brings you the final part of her
MEDITERRANEAN BRIDES duet, *Taken: The Spaniard's
Virgin*, where Miguel takes Amber's innocence. There's
another sexy Spaniard in Trish Morey's *The Spaniard's
Blackmailed Bride*, when Blair is blackmailed into
marriage but Diablo's touch sets her body on fire!
In *Bought for the Greek's Bed* by Julia James,
Theo demands his new bride also be his wife in the
bedroom. In *The Greek Millionaire's Mistress* by
Catherine Spencer, Gina Hudson goes to settle an old
score in Athens, only to fall into the arms—and bed!—
of a tycoon. *The Sicilian's Red-Hot Revenge* by
Kate Walker has a handsome, fiery Italian who wants
revenge, but what happens when he discovers he's
going to be a father? In Annie West's *The Sheikh's
Ransomed Bride*, powerful Sheikh Rafiq rescues Belle
from rebels, only to demand marriage in return! And in
Maggie Cox's *The Millionaire Boss's Baby*, a brooding
boss's sensual seduction proves too good to resist.
Enjoy!

Mediterranean Brides

Two billionaires, one Greek, one Spanish—
will they tame their unwilling wives?

Meet Sandor and Miguel, men who've taken
all the prizes when it comes to looks, power,
wealth and arrogance. Now they want marriage
with two beautiful women. But this time, for
the first time, both Mediterranean billionaires
have met their matches and it will take
more than money or cool to tame their
unwilling mistresses—try seduction,
passion and possession!

The MEDITERRANEAN BRIDES duet:

Bought: The Greek's Bride
Sandor's story

Taken: The Spaniard's Virgin
Miguel's story

Available this month

Lucy Monroe

TAKEN:
THE SPANIARD'S VIRGIN

Mediterranean Brides

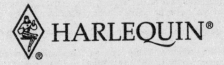

HARLEQUIN®

TORONTO • NEW YORK • LONDON
AMSTERDAM • PARIS • SYDNEY • HAMBURG
STOCKHOLM • ATHENS • TOKYO • MILAN • MADRID
PRAGUE • WARSAW • BUDAPEST • AUCKLAND

ISBN-13: 978-0-373-23408-0
ISBN-10: 0-373-23408-2

TAKEN: THE SPANIARD'S VIRGIN

First North American Publication 2007.

Copyright © 2007 by Lucy Monroe.

This edition published by arrangement with Harlequin Books S.A.

® and TM are trademarks of the publisher. Trademarks indicated with ® are registered in the United States Patent and Trademark Office, the Canadian Trade Marks Office and in other countries.

www.eHarlequin.com

Printed in U.S.A.

All about the author...
Lucy Monroe

LUCY MONROE sold her first book in
September 2002 to the Harlequin Presents line.
That book represented a dream that had been
burning in her heart for years: the dream to share
her stories with readers who love romance as
much as she does. Since then she has sold more
than thirty books to three publishers and hit
national bestseller lists in the U.S. and England.
But since selling that first book, the reader letters
she receives have touched her most deeply. Her
most important goal with every book is to touch
a reader's heart, and it is this connection that makes
those nights spent writing into the wee hours
worth it.

She started reading Harlequin Presents books
very young and discovered a heroic type of man
between the covers of those books—an honorable
man, capable of faithfulness and sacrifice for the
people he loves. Now married to what she terms
her "alpha male at the end of a book," Lucy believes
there is a lot more reality to the fantasy stories she
writes than most people give credit for. She believes
happy endings are really marvelous beginnings
and that's why she writes them. She hopes her
books help readers to believe a little, too...just like
romance did for her so many years ago.

Lucy enjoys hearing from readers and responds
to every e-mail. You can reach her by e-mailing
lucymonroe@lucymonroe.com.

For my readers. I write to share the stories in my heart with the special group of people whose hearts are open to them—my readers. I thank God for each and every one of you. Knowing you are buying and reading my books touches me to the tips of my soul. Your e-mails make my day and your love for romance and my stories keep me writing! THANK YOU!

Blessings and much love, Lucy—
lucymonroe@lucymonroe.com

CHAPTER ONE

"DROP your head a little to the left. That's right. Good, Amber, good."

Amber Taylor moved to the direction of the photographer, the hot Spanish sun baking her skin despite the high factor sunscreen slathered on under her body sheen. She didn't complain, though. The shoot was her first truly big ad campaign as well as her first large international contract.

At twenty-four, she was either on the cusp of making it big in modeling, or sliding into mediocrity. Mediocrity was not an option. She'd been modeling since her early teens and had sacrificed sleep, chocolate and a social life for her chosen career. She was determined to make it big.

It helped that her mom was on her side. A widow, who had raised Amber on her own, Helen Taylor was an amazing woman. She'd sacrificed herself for Amber's career and loved her only daughter enough to remind her when to exercise and when *not* to eat… too much.

Amber had been living on a low-calorie diet so long, she didn't even get hungry anymore. Helen was careful to make sure that the food Amber did eat was übernutritious. She'd even given up her own comforts so that she could afford to hire a personal trainer for Amber. Helen Taylor had provided Amber what she needed to hone her body into the perfect form for modeling.

Her mom's support of her dream meant everything to Amber and she had every intention of repaying it with success.

"Okay…lift the phone like a victory fist and smile."

Amber lifted the trim flip phone high in the air and gave her signature smile, one that her agent said promised the world and everything in it.

A whistle sounded from her left and unexpected tingles traveled up her spine and down her arms. It was if someone with an electric gaze was watching her. Which was just plain silly. Superman might have X-ray vision, but he was fiction and no real person actually had the ability to touch someone else with a look. Only, she felt touched. Caressed even.

Doing her best to mentally shrug off the odd feeling, she turned up the wattage on her smile and the whistle sounded again. This time low and suggestive. It was all Amber could do not to clench her thigh muscles. She never reacted like this.

Never.

A swear word hissed out between her perfect teeth even as she maintained the smile for the numerous clicks of the photographer's camera. What was wrong with her?

"Call a break." The voice rang with authority and just the hint of a Castilian accent.

The photographer called the break and Amber dropped the cell phone she'd been holding onto a nearby table. She went to pull on a gauzy wrap, but two elegant, masculine hands were there before hers.

The wrap was held open waiting for her to slide her arms into it. "Come, *querida*, you must cover such perfect skin from the heat of the sun."

She allowed him to draw the wrap up her arms, a sense of unreality stifling her. She had not even seen his face yet and felt as if they were intimately acquainted. Impossible.

And just slightly terrifying.

"Whose not so brilliant idea was it to work during the hottest part of the day?" he asked in a voice that carried as far as the photographer.

"It is the light, Señor Menendez. It is perfect right now," the ad campaign manager said in a much less authoritative voice than Amber had ever heard from him while she saw the photographer hurry over out of the corner of her eye.

"Are we not civilized? Does not the siesta demand rest, not work during the hottest part of the day?"

"I apologize, señor. If we had known you wished to oversee the shoot, we would have arranged it for a different time."

The man behind Amber laughed, the sound warm and rich, like chocolate sauce pouring over French vanilla ice cream. "It is not myself I am concerned about."

That strange urge to clench her thigh muscles hit her again and she had to force herself to step out from under the hands now resting on her shoulders. When had she ever wanted to prolong a man's touch? She could not remember a single instance. Men were business associates or props for photo shoots, nothing more.

She turned to face the man upsetting her equilibrium and got her first glimpse of Señor Miguel Menendez. Her brain immediately began to catalog the information she had on him.

His family ran Menendez Industries, the parent corporation for the cell phone company doing the ad campaign she was posing for. While his grandfather and father still played an active role in running the business, analysts agreed that Miguel was responsible for most of Menendez Industries' expansion in the last five years.

He'd gotten them in at ground level with cell phone service to parts of Asia and Europe as well as negotiating investment in other high tech ventures that had paid off hugely for the more than hundred-year-old, multibillion dollar, family controlled company. He wasn't the only member of his generation involved with the company, but thus far, he'd been the most successful.

Amber had done her homework, learning what she could about both the company and product she was supposed to be representing—as she always did for a job. As her mom often said, it never hurt to be prepared. Only she had the distinct feeling that nothing could have equipped her for seeing the billionaire in person for the first time.

She'd seen photos, but the pictures accompanying articles in prominent business journals hadn't begun to catch the essence of the man. The flat two-dimensional images had in no way alluded to his sheer animal magnetism or overwhelming masculine presence.

Six feet two inches of prime male, Miguel Menendez had a body most male models would have sacrificed a year's wages for. Tall, lean and muscular, he filled out his Dolce & Gabbana shirt and trousers like they'd been made for him. And they probably had. While she recognized the cut and style of the designer's signature look, there were subtle differences that implied this man's clothes weren't even bought off the runway.

Not that a super rich tycoon was going to do anything but have a personal shopper who brought designers to him, but still.

Gray eyes watched her with heated interest tempered by a humor that surprised her. The man made her go weak in the knees and considering she spent her time with some of the most beautiful males the earth had to offer on a regular basis, that realization was not an altogether welcome one.

Yes, his patrician features and dark, curling hair were to-die-for gorgeous, but it was more than that. And it was the *more* that had her taking another step backward in the awkward silence that had fallen after his last statement.

He smiled, even white teeth flashing briefly. "My concern is for this most lovely young woman whose beauty will not be enhanced by sunburn I think."

"We've got Amber slathered in fifty factor sunscreen," the photographer said dismissively.

Señor Menendez's eyes narrowed. "I see that you are in long sleeves and wearing a hat. Very sensible…while she pretends to talk on the phone in little more than three triangles of fabric."

"She's a model."

Which said it all. Her body was a tool. To sell products for them and to achieve her dreams for Amber. It was the way it was and she didn't even mind.

But apparently Señor Menendez did. She could only be grateful she was not the recipient of that particular look. The photographer tugged at his collar and looked beseechingly at the ad campaign manager who in turn was looking at his boss as if the tycoon had sprouted a couple of horns.

"She is a beautiful woman whom you would do better to care for than to mistreat in such a manner if indeed it is her image we wish to use to encourage customers to use our products." He turned to her, the chilled visage warming. "Though I am still unsure of what a barely clad woman and better cell phone coverage have in common."

She laughed, charmed by his blatant bemusement. "My body has been used to sell car batteries. I'm not really sure what the connection is, but I'm personally grateful advertisers seem to think there's a correlation. And honestly…I've done photo shoots in the California desert during the summer. This isn't any worse. Believe me."

A smile flirted at the edges of his perfectly shaped lips. "But we are more civilized than Californians, yes?"

"If you say so." She'd found that some

Europeans still saw Americans as back-woodsmen.

Her agent would swoon at being described in such a way, but Perry had a propensity for drama anyway.

Señor Menendez cocked his head. "You said your *body*?"

She shrugged.

"Surely *you* sell the products."

"My image, which is essentially my body."

He shook his head decisively. "No. There are thousands of truly beautiful women who could be standing where you are right now, it is the spirit inside you that shines through when you smile as you were doing when I arrived. It is *you* that my advertising executives hired…not a mere body."

He was right. Modeling was so much more than displaying body parts to their best advantage, but few people saw it that way. And regardless, her body was still the main tool for her trade. Which sounded kind of bad when she thought of it and didn't open her mouth to say so.

She simply smiled and said, "Thank you."

"The smile…it is real? Or can you turn it on for others as well as the camera?"

The question was like a smack between the eyes. It was too much like the question that had been plaguing her lately. Was she a plastic person, or real? Sometimes she felt like a wind-up toy that operated only for the photographer's pull on her string. She'd always worked hard to be in charge of her career, but was it really controlling her?

"When was the last time you did something for the sake of enjoyment alone?" he asked although she had not answered his first question yet.

"I…" She didn't remember. Maybe if her mom were here, she could ask her.

While she was Amber's biggest supporter for her career, her mom still pushed Amber to relax occasionally, reminding her that life wasn't all about modeling. But she still couldn't think of a recent time when it hadn't been.

She stood there, feeling exposed and vulnerable. There was only one safe place of retreat. Behind the plastic smile.

She flashed it. "My career is all the fun I need, Señor Menendez. Now, if you gentlemen don't mind, I'd like a chance to get a drink before we resume shooting."

He reached out and caught her arm before she walked away. "Let me buy you a fruit juice. And my name is Miguel. Use it."

He dismissed the other two men with a jerk of his head and the ad campaign manager and photographer melted away.

"Is that an order?" she asked, her internal hackles rising as she once again faced him.

While her body might be her tool for her trade, it was not a plaything and if he thought she'd fit the role of a playboy's plaything in her off-hours, he was very much mistaken.

"Does it need to be?" he countered, ignoring the frost in her voice.

"That depends. Do your other employees call you by your first name?"

"Some do. Some don't. I prefer that you do. And technically, you are not my employee, but a private contractor hired for a specific purpose. Quite outside my jurisdiction."

"So outside of your jurisdiction that you called a break in the middle of a successful shoot and have dismissed the two men I *do* answer to in order to be alone with me?"

He shrugged.

"I don't think anything in *any* of your companies is truly outside your jurisdiction,

Miguel...except me." There was no warmth in the smile that curved her lips then. "I'm a model, not an escort."

Undaunted, he gave her a genuine grin, his gray eyes filled with amusement and unalloyed approval. "You are a beautiful woman I wish to get to know. What is the harm in that?"

"You tell me."

"You are very prickly, are you not?"

"I've learned to be."

"Have a glass of fruit juice with me. Decide if you like my company enough to share dinner tonight."

She opened her mouth to deny him, but he put a finger to her lips.

"A moment of your time only. Please."

This was not a man who said that particular word very often. She was certain of it.

She shut her mouth.

He left his hand where it was. "Your decision will in no way impact your role as cover model for this campaign."

She stared at him, trying to read his sincerity. All the articles she'd read about him touted him as an honest man. And fair. She chose to believe.

She couldn't talk with his finger pressed

against her lips, however. Well, she could, but she was finding it difficult enough to deal with the sensations that tiny touch evoked without moving her lips against him. She swallowed and nodded with a short jerk of her head.

He smiled and let his hand drop. "Good."

The photo shoot was being done on a roped off area of the beach and he led her to a small café less than twenty yards from it. They took a table for two outside and he called the waiter with an arrogant flick of his hand.

The young man came over, his eyes widened as if in recognition. She supposed the billionaire was something of a celebrity in his home country...like Hollywood actors back home. But Miguel Menendez was a lot better looking. Miguel ordered them both a glass of fruit juice before she could think better of it and request water. The extra electrolytes wouldn't hurt and she could make up for it by eating less at dinner, she thought with a mental shrug, unconsciously counting the calories.

"Have you always wanted to be a model?" he asked after the waiter left.

"Yes. How about you? Have you always wanted to be a business tycoon?"

He laughed, the sound running along her nerve endings like a hypercharged current. "I was born to it, more or less. My father was a businessman and his father before him. You know the story."

"But you've taken the family holdings to unprecedented heights."

It was his turn to look wary. "Reading the gossip rags?"

"Business weeklies actually. My mother's a financial consultant and she raised me on bedtime stories where the Big Bad Wolf was a guy selling junk bonds and Prince Charming was a good investment partner."

Now, his gaze turned speculative. "I am surprised you chose the career you did then."

"Why? I invested in a personal asset I could enhance at will…my looks. I have worked my tail off to make them pay dividends and they have. That's a better investment than many business ventures over which I would have less control regarding the principle component my success would depend on."

"Have the dividends been worth the hard work?" he asked, his tone laced with reluctant respect.

"You tell me. Have your sacrifices been worth the business success?"

"Yes. What is a twenty-hour workday compared to my family's security?"

She liked that he thought in terms of family commitment. She only had her mom, but they were devoted to each other. Family came first. She sipped at her juice. "Thankfully, since graduating from university two years ago, I don't have to work twenty-hour days any longer."

"You went to university?"

"That surprises you?"

"Considering your dedication to your career, yes. The time and cost of your education would have taken a toll on what is clearly your main goal in life."

"I saw it that way, but Mom didn't. She has always supported my desire to be a model, but no model's career lasts forever and she maintained the better education I had, the better I would be at managing my career."

"Is that not what an agent is for?"

"A model who leaves her career to others is just looking for a trap door in the floor to fall through to obscurity."

"That sounds like a well-rehearsed rule."

"It is."

The warmth and approval were there again in his gaze. "I like you, Amber."

"I think I could like you, too, Miguel."

"Only think?"

"I'm the cautious type."

He threw his head back and laughed.

And something inside, suspiciously near her heart, melted.

He was there when the shoot finished two hours later.

He'd been there the whole time, watching, asking questions of the ad campaign manager, of the photographer and even one or two questions of her. Was the ground too hot for her bare feet? He hadn't believed her when she said no and his displeasure at her supposed discomfort had been obvious. So much so that they'd quickly moved to a different shot. Then he'd asked what she'd thought of the ad campaign.

She'd requested a water break to tell him. She was impressed with the ad designer's vision and thought the campaign would be effective and didn't mind saying so.

"You've studied the market?"

"If your job was to represent it, wouldn't you?"

"Yes, I suppose I would." He picked up the spray-on sunscreen and started to mist her with it. "You continually surprise me, Amber. It is a new experience for me with a woman."

"You must be spending time with the wrong ones."

"I think that is a given." He winked.

Her heart stopped. Literally. And then started pounding so hard and fast, she felt light-headed. This man was so bad for her equilibrium. "I need to get back to work," she said, only sounding a tiny bit breathless.

"Have dinner with me tonight."

She'd been surprised he hadn't pushed the issue earlier, but the man knew his way around women. He'd given her time to think, time to decide if she wanted to see him some more. He'd dialed in right away that control was important to her and having time to make a decision would make her feel like she wasn't losing it. His perception should worry her, but she was too busy experiencing new feelings.

Not just the desire that was such an incredibly different thing for her, but weird emotions, too. She really liked Miguel

Menendez. He got to the heart of the woman that hid behind the plastic smile.

It was both scary and very, very exhilarating.

"Okay," she heard herself saying with a sense of fatalism that was also new to her. "But the shoot tomorrow starts before the cock crows. I need to be in my suite early."

"I am happy to make sure you get to bed early if that is what you want."

CHAPTER TWO

SHE'D be naive to think he meant anything innocent by that remark and she might be inexperienced, but she was far from naive. She frowned accordingly.

But that only made him smile. "You are cute when you are trying to look angry."

She couldn't remember the last time someone had called her cute. Not since she was a child...before she developed the poised bearing of a professional model. It was strangely endearing. Too much about this man got to her in ways that were risky for her peace of mind.

"Believe me, when I'm trying to look mad...I do."

His dark brow rose in mocking amusement. "If you say so."

"Don't make the mistake of patronizing me." She drank from her bottle of chilled water.

"I would not."

"I'm no pushover, Miguel."

"This I have no difficulty believing."

That made her feel a little better. "I need to get back."

"I will pick you up at six for an early dinner."

"I didn't know any restaurants served dinner that early around here."

"I will take care of it."

She supposed billionaire tycoons got fed wherever they wanted, whenever they wanted. "Okay."

Then he'd let her get back to work, but he hadn't left.

The photographer called an end to the shoot and Miguel was there with a floor-length, long-sleeved, light cotton white robe that would protect her from the sun instantly. She wondered vaguely where it had come from, but didn't hesitate to pull it on. Her skin didn't need the baking rays of the sun on it any longer than absolutely necessary.

Her flawless, youthful complexion was one of her trademarks.

The photographer winked at her before leaving. The ad design manager smiled at her and nodded toward Miguel before he, too, left. At least neither man seemed angry she'd caught the attention of the mogul. On the other hand, *was* that a good thing? Were these people so used to seeing Miguel make a play for their ad models that they took it in stride?

"You are frowning again, looking infinitely more disturbed than you were earlier." He adjusted the robe on her shoulders, his gaze concerned if she could make herself believe it.

Cinching the robe tighter, she asked, "Do you hit on all the models that get hired by your ad department?"

"My company is far too big for me to oversee every photo shoot and not all cover models are female. I have definite heterosexual biases," he joked.

Her stomach plummeted. Misdirection was not the same thing as a denial and she needed solid denial to feel even sort of good about going out with him. "I think we'd better give dinner a miss."

"Do not be ridiculous." Irritation laced his voice. "Do you seriously believe I need my ad department to find me dates?"

"No, but that doesn't mean you don't take advantage of the situation."

"You are truly bothered by this?"

"Yes."

He called the ad campaign manager, who had just exited the small trailer he'd been using as headquarters for the shoot, over. "Stephan."

The other man hitched his satchel on his shoulder, obviously ready to leave the remaining break down to the technicians. "Yes, señor?"

"Tell Miss Taylor how often I have hit on models employed by our company." His voice had chilled with distaste on the words *hit on*.

Stephan measured her with his eyes, his dark gaze clearly filled with surprise. Whether it was surprise that she would have the temerity to question his super powerful employer or at the question itself, she did not know.

"Never that I have seen, señor," he said with either genuine sincerity or a very good approximation of it.

Heat scorched up her neck into her cheeks. "It doesn't matter. I still don't think this is a good idea." She fluttered her hands, indicating them.

Miguel dismissed his employee with a look and then turned to her, his expression hard and not at all potential-loverlike. "I think it is a very good idea and so do you, but for some reason you are afraid. I assure you, you have no reason to be."

"You're a bad risk for a woman like me. I think, honestly, that you are a bad risk period."

The words should have offended him, but they didn't. His smile was back. "Life would be very boring without risk, do you not agree?"

He hadn't even bothered to try to deny it. But then, even the business journals alluded to a love 'em and leave 'em reputation for him. "Maybe, but some risks are worse than others."

"And some pay off in dividends that are unimaginable."

"You think dinner with you falls in that category?"

"I guarantee it."

"Arrogant."

"Confident."

"With you, it's the same thing."

He laughed again and she capitulated. "Okay, dinner. But you aren't putting me to bed, early or otherwise," she warned him.

"Duly noted." He smiled and her inner woman actually rocked back on her heels. "May I see you home?"

"I can take a taxi."

"There is no need. I have my car at your disposal."

"I suppose that would be all right."

"Such enthusiasm."

She crossed her arms and tilted her head back to meet his eyes dead-on. "I would think you get enough sycophantic behavior from others."

His lips quirked. "Touché."

"Give me a second to put my clothes on and I'll be ready to go." The bikini covered less than most of her undergarments and no way was she riding back to her hotel clad in it, or even the robe he'd found somewhere for her.

"No problem."

It didn't take her long to change into the short white crocheted Lilly Pulitzer dress and flat silver sandals she'd worn on arrival to the shoot. Even fully lined, the dress was comfortably lightweight for the intense Spanish summer heat. She ran a brush through her shoulder-length, professionally highlighted hair and smeared some clear gloss onto her chapping lips. Miguel had been right about one thing. It had been a very hot shoot.

Grabbing her bag, she went to join him. She hurried and marveled at the feeling like she needed to do so. *She wanted to be with him.* It was a heady and nerve-racking sensation. Her mom had warned her it could happen like this, but Amber had always thought she was immune. She'd never been in love and frankly, considering the way her mom still grieved the loss of her dad before she was ever born, she didn't crave the intense emotion, either.

She'd always been happy. Content. She had a super demanding career which she adored. A couple of good friends, though she saw them infrequently. One was a fellow model and the other she'd met at college. She and her mom were close.

She dated, albeit rarely, but she didn't need a man in her life. He would just mess things up. Particularly a man like Miguel. He would expect her to make concessions for him. Would he reciprocate, though?

She tried to convince herself she was getting ahead of herself, but deep down inside, she knew she wasn't. This man spelled trouble in her life in capital letters. So, why was she rushing to meet him?

Because like he'd said…some risks were worth the trouble.

* * *

He drove a black Ferrari like he'd taken training with the Andretti family. And yet she never felt at risk, never felt like he drove recklessly. Just very fast and with tons of confidence.

In fact, she kind of liked it. For a woman who never drove over the speed limit herself and actually drove as little as possible, but when she did...it was always very cautiously—it was an odd sort of pleasure. But it was indisputably pleasure nevertheless.

"So, have you enjoyed your time in Barcelona?" he asked as he shifted gears.

"Yes. I haven't done a lot of international travel, so it's been something of a perk doing this shoot."

"It is one of your bigger campaigns, yes?"

"Did you do your homework while I was busy posing for the camera?"

"I made a phone call or two."

That didn't surprise her. "And what did you find out?"

"Enough."

She turned in her seat to face him. "What does that mean?"

"I am very attracted to you."

"I got that impression."

"I have to be careful of the women I date."

"Are you saying you had a quick rundown on my character investigated?"

"In essence, yes."

"Wow. I don't think I've ever been investigated by a potential date before." She wasn't sure how she felt about that.

"It was hardly a major investigation."

"How could it be? Your investigator only had a couple of hours."

His long brown fingers curled around the steering wheel like they were an extension of it. "He had long enough to determine that you don't make it a habit to date wealthy men and file lawsuits for support after. In point of fact, he saw little evidence of you dating at all."

It wasn't a question, but she could feel him waiting for her response all the same.

"Fishing?" she asked, trying to determine if she was offended that he'd had her checked out on the premise he mentioned. She supposed that a man with his wealth had to be careful, but it still felt strange in a not so nice way.

"Maybe. You are too beautiful not to have frequent dates."

Definitely fishing. "You don't sound like you trust your investigator's report."

"Maybe I am simply curious about you."

There was a level of sincerity in his tone that struck a similar chord in her.

"Most men who ask a model out are looking for adornment. That role leaves me cold."

"You have decided I did not request your company with such shallow motives?" He sounded pleased by the prospect.

"Fairly confident, but the truth is…I didn't even think about it this time." There was such a thing as being too honest.

So, why did she feel compelled to open her mouth and spit out potentially embarrassing truths with this man? All of her usual reactions were off with Miguel. He drew too much from her. Too much honesty. Too much physical response. Too much everything.

"You feel it as well." He didn't sound happy, so much as confused. Perhaps his reaction to her was just as out of the ordinary for him.

It was a comforting scenario, so she decided to stick with it. "What exactly do you think I'm feeling?" she probed.

"This thing between us." One hand came off the steering wheel to gesture between them.

"The attraction." She wasn't sure what else to label it.

"I would call it super attraction." He shook

his head. "I have not reacted to a woman like this since I was a young man. Do not think I make it habit of using company resources to run instant background checks on women. I am not usually so impatient."

"I know what you mean." Relief flooded her that her comfort scenario was more reality than fantasy. He felt how big the thing was between them just like she did. "It's more than attraction."

"Yes."

Another good answer.

"So, what do we do about it?"

"You have to ask?"

"I'm not one for falling into bed on a first date." Or any date, but that wasn't something she needed to mention right now.

He cast her a sidelong glance from his gray eyes. "Let us enjoy one another's company and see where it goes."

"I've never been very good at taking things as they come."

"It is always good to try new things."

"My agent says the same thing…usually when he's trying to talk me into doing a spread I'm going to hate."

It came again, that laughter that made

her insides melt. "I assure you, I am not luring you into something you will hate. Quite the opposite."

She had a feeling he did not know how right he was. She very much feared Miguel Menendez was a man she could love.

Miguel turned off the car in the valet circle for Amber's hotel. "I do not want to leave you."

The beautiful woman beside him jolted as if he'd shocked her.

Hell, he'd shocked himself. He sounded like a needy adolescent, but he only had a few weeks before he flew out for Prague. He hoped to convince Amber to spend as much of that time with him as possible. He had already confirmed with her agent that after the shoot for his company was done, she planned to spend a week in Spain on holiday.

He had every intention of taking advantage of that fact, but each moment in Amber's company had reiterated to him how important her career was. No way would she take a sabbatical to go with him to Prague. And why he was even considering such a possibility, he could not fathom. Women were not permanent fixtures in his life. No woman had even made the status of semi-long-term.

He enjoyed feminine companionship and sex was important to him, but he had never wanted to keep a woman in his life before. Now was really no different. He simply felt a stronger physical attraction to Amber than he had to another woman in so long, he couldn't remember another time. Once they sated their mutual desire, these strange thoughts of togetherness would no doubt pass.

She ran her hands through her multicolored blond hair, messing it up sexily and his libido surged. "I need a shower."

"You have a suite."

"You want to come up?" Her aquamarine eyes doubted the viability of that suggestion.

He had no doubts. "Yes."

She bit her lip and looked away, the gesture at odds with the sophisticated woman he knew her to be. "I suppose that would be all right."

She sounded unsure…innocent. That turned him on in ways it probably shouldn't. He'd dated many women from her world, just none that had been contracted to work for his company. It was not a world where innocence or uncertainty lasted long. She'd come too far to be either of those things, but he enjoyed the illusion. And best of all, he didn't think she was projecting it on purpose.

She was as affected by their meeting as he had been and it made her vulnerable. Why that was so appealing he did not know, but it was.

She looked nervously at him. He smiled, though he doubted his expression was reassuring. He was too hungry for her. Getting out of the car, he considered the possibility that she was playing him rather than honestly vulnerable and dismissed it.

The vulnerability was real, but the rest might be the behavior of a master tactician. She had the reluctant interest bit down pat anyway. No chance was she sincerely as reticent about going out with him as she had acted. Yes, the beguiling Amber Taylor knew exactly how to increase interest in a man like him. Underneath civilization's veneer, he was a predator at heart. Skittish prey only made him more determined to succeed in the chase.

He thought he had been played by the best, but this woman was light years beyond the average female in securing his attention. And he didn't mind at all. In fact, he admired her.

She was also clearly a master at discretion. Even when he'd subtly quizzed her, she had been adept at sidestepping his inquiry about her dating habits rather than answering them. As he would expect if she was used to dating men in prominent positions. With her beauty and intelligence, he had no doubt she was. However, Miguel's investigator was fairly confident she was not involved in a relationship currently.

She'd been telling the truth when she said she worked hard and if not twenty-hour workdays, long ones all the same. She'd had back-to-back jobs for the past several months. No man in his position would tolerate his woman being quite that unavailable.

She had to be unattached at the moment.

Both his brain and his libido insisted on it.

The libido taking precedence as he touched her hand to help her from the car. "Thank you for not sending me away."

Her gaze slipped up to meet his as her hand seemed to flutter against his, her perfect oval features set in an indecipherable expression. "If you want the truth, I feel the same…" She paused as if looking for the word. "Greedy desire for your company."

He liked hearing that far more than he

would have expected. And it didn't fit the "playing hard to get" role she'd been in earlier, either. There was a gut level honesty to this woman that years working in her cut-throat industry had not been able to beat out of her. He liked that. He liked it a lot.

He smiled and took her well-toned, honey gold arm in his. "What floor are you staying on?"

The woman's body was as close to perfect as it was possible to get without plastic augmentation and she was too genuine to be the result of cosmetic surgery.

Her eyes opened wide in mock surprise. "Are you saying your sources have not already supplied you with that knowledge?"

"Actually, no, they haven't." He hadn't thought to ask. It had never occurred to him that she wouldn't offer it.

"You'll have to chastise them for being behind the ball on that one."

"Considering the fact that my company booked your rooms, you are right. It would have been all too easy to come by the information." If he had asked.

"Exactly."

He shook his head.

The airy hotel lobby was starting to grow busy now that the hours for siesta were past. He saw more than one person do a double-take when they spied him walking with Amber. He sighed. There was no hope of keeping his relationship with her a complete secret, not in his hometown. But he had already instructed his company and anyone who had worked with Amber since she came to Spain to remain mute on her identity when the inevitable queries began to arise.

His family strictly enforced the policy that any employee who thought a bribe was worth betraying a Menendez's privacy to the media would be looking for another job the minute the perfidy was discovered. Subsequently the press leaks from within the conglomeration were extremely rare and his family enjoyed a deeper level of privacy than most in their social and economic position.

He guided Amber into the elevator, shielding her body with his own from curious eyes. "It is inevitable that photos of us will make it into the scandal rags, but I have taken steps to protect your privacy."

"Thank you."

"You do not want the free publicity?"

She shook her head decisively. "I am no more interested in seeing my date as a trophy on my arm than I am in being one myself."

"I approve your stance."

She grinned at him. "Thanks. Are you often considered a trophy?"

"I tend to avoid certain relationships and therefore the possibility, but sometimes the exchange is worth it."

"Sex for temporary access to your wealth and position?"

"As long as they understand it is temporary, it works."

"That's very cold."

"I do not see it that way."

"It makes the women you share your bed with little more than paid companions."

"What a subtle turn of phrase, but the choice to trade on sexual compatibility is theirs not mine. I do not make them anything."

"But your attitude encourages it."

"I assure you, a woman must convince me it is worth my time to be used as her temporary ticket into a certain lifestyle."

"But you let yourself be convinced."

"Yes." There was no use denying it. Not that he wanted to. His life was what it was.

He had accepted that long ago. "We have already decided that such an exchange is not the driving force behind what is happening between us, have we not?"

The elevator dinged and the doors slid open. He guided her out into the hall, keeping his hand on her arm.

She slid a sideways look at him, biting her lip in that endearing way again. "I'm not sure how I feel about being with a man who admits to having relationships of that sort even if he wants me to believe ours won't follow the same pattern."

"First, we have both acknowledged we are not looking for a trophy, yes?"

"Yes."

"Second, would you prefer I pretend to be someone different?"

"No, I just…"

"Accept that I left naive idealism behind in the nursery."

She stopped in front of a door and pulled her key card out. "I do not consider respect for my sex naive."

"I respect women."

She pushed the door open and stepped inside. "Really?"

He followed her, pushing the door closed behind him. "Yes. I respect women enough to believe they are capable of deciding what sort of relationship is best for them."

CHAPTER THREE

HE SHRUGGED out of his jacket and laid it over the back of one of two armchairs on either side of a small, low table. The suite wasn't as spacious as his usual accommodations, but it was modern and decently decorated. And it was a true suite with a door between the bedroom and the tiny living area. He would expect no less from his company.

She had stopped at the door leading to the bedroom, and stood there appearing somewhat agitated. "I could never settle for something so cold."

"I accept that."

"So, what do you expect the exchange between us to be?"

"I want you. You want me. It is entirely mutual." In his mind, it needed no further definition.

"And not mercenary."

"In no way mercenary. On either side. I want you for more than arm ornamentation." Though some might call his dead-on rush at her knowing the relationship could only last a matter of weeks mercenary, he did not consider it that way. Relationships never lasted longer than that for him and he had done nothing to encourage her to expect anything different.

In fact, he had emphasized the temporary nature of his previous affairs and while she had not liked his blunt view of them, she had not argued that aspect to them.

"And I am not looking to spend your money or for you to advance my career."

"See? Nothing cold about it." He had caught on rather quickly that was important to the aqua-eyed beauty before him.

"Definitely not cold." She smiled.

And he had to stifle a growl of desire. Scorching heat was a better description of what was between them.

A growing erection pressed against his tailored slacks while his hands itched to touch her silky, golden skin. *Want* was a tame word for the feelings crashing through him. He *craved* that too kissable mouth, hungered for it like a man starved. He *needed* to taste her delectable lips…and everywhere else.

He did not like this needing. He had to get her to bed soon to gain control of the wayward feeling. He did not respond this way to women. Ever. It took more than physical beauty to draw him. Yet he could hardly claim to know Amber as well as he usually did a woman he wanted to bed. Though each moment spent in her company revealed an intelligence and charm that increased the aching desire in his sex. And there was no denying that he wanted to bed her. Very soon. Over and over again.

She put her hand on the doorknob. "I'm going to go take my shower."

"I will catch up on phone calls while you are getting ready. Do not rush yourself."

She smiled and nodded.

He pulled out his cell phone and dialed the investigator to see if he had anything more and refused to question why he would do so when he had other more pressing calls to make.

Miguel was talking to an associate in China when Amber walked out of the bedroom. Several years of training not to show emotion during business negotiations were all that prevented him from embarrassing himself.

"You look breathtaking," he mouthed while the Chinese businessman on the other end of his phone call rattled off statistics none the wiser.

Her golden highlighted hair hung down like a curtain of spun silk framing her exquisitely shaped face. She'd donned another dress, but this one was the same color as her eyes and clung lovingly to her slim curves, accentuating both how very tiny she was for her height and how deeply feminine.

Her feet were encased in delicate gold sandals that added a good three inches to her height. She'd been wearing flats earlier. It pleased him that she'd dressed up for him.

Her jewelry looked like it had been designed by Aztecs. It was an interesting choice and spoke of a woman not afraid to draw attention to herself. Which made perfect sense considering the profession she was in, but he still liked the evidence of her confidence.

He'd never found timidity attractive, not like some of the other men in his family who seemed to thrive on the different kind of chase. Give him a lioness over a kitten anyday.

Enchantingly, Amber blushed. "Thank you," she mouthed back.

He nodded, not taking his eyes off of her though he did manage to return part of his brain to the business discussion. A very small part.

Amber crossed to the mini bar and poured herself a glass of bottled water. She turned to him, lifting her brow in question.

He shook his head. He'd already raided the drinks fridge and finished off a bottle of water and a small Coke while making his phone calls.

She drank her water while he talked to the other man, seemingly indifferent to the fact that he was otherwise occupied. He liked that, too.

Most women he'd dated were impatient with his need to conduct business at odd hours and sometimes inopportune moments. He finished up the call and then flipped his phone shut. "Thank you for your patience."

"No problem." She smiled. "I'm glad you weren't in here pacing the room waiting for me to finish getting ready."

He packed the papers back into the briefcase he'd brought from his car. "By rights, I should have left you and returned later for dinner."

"But you didn't want to leave." She moved to lean against the arm of the chair opposite the one he was sitting in.

"No."

"This feels strange to me."

"Ditto."

She smiled wryly. "I figured. I wasn't expecting to meet someone like you when I was here. I thought it would just be another job."

"I do not think you can ever be prepared for the kind of attraction we feel."

Her aquamarine eyes flared briefly with something that looked like relief. "No, I'm sure you can't."

He stood, moving closer to her and reached down to cup her shoulder. "I like the way you make me feel."

"Do you?"

"Yes."

"I wouldn't have pegged you for a man who likes being out of control."

"I am not out of control." But her words pricked his conscience. He hadn't liked realizing what he felt for her bordered on need rather than desire.

"Aren't you?"

"No." He was not quite to that point.

"Did you intend to spend the day overseeing the shoot?" she asked innocently, but he knew what she was getting at.

He grimaced in wry acknowledgment of the hit. "No."

"And you've already admitted you should have gone back to your office rather than staying here with me."

"Your point?" But he knew what it was, only *she* wasn't looking at the whole picture.

"Call me crazy, but that doesn't sound like the actions of a man completely in control."

That was where she was wrong. He had been in control because the choices had been his. "I saw you. It was like being hit by a bullet train. I decided to pursue the attraction. But I *chose* to change my schedule to accommodate my desire. Me. In control."

And hadn't he managed to finish his business discussion rather than hanging up like he'd wanted to and kissing her until they were both naked and writhing on the floor? But when was the last time he'd contemplated making love on the floor?

Dios. "Maybe I feel a little out of control, but I'm managing." Who was he trying to convince? Her, or himself?

"I'm glad someone is," she muttered under her breath, looking away. Her body language changed subtly.

An arm crossed over her waist, her hand clasping the elbow of the arm that held her drink as she moved to sit in the armchair, creating a small barrier between them. Her legs crossed elegantly, pointed just slightly away from him and in the space of two seconds, she went from being open and warm to wary and reserved.

He'd lost ground. Not sure how or why, he only knew he didn't like it.

He leaned over and tipped her face toward him with his thumb against her chin. "What is the matter?"

She gave him the smile he'd already learned to associate with her public persona. "Nothing."

"Do not lie to me. Ever."

She measured him with her eyes until he released her chin. Then she spoke. "*I* don't feel in control. It took major self-discipline not to rush through getting ready so I could get back to you. I even considered not washing my hair to cut out the drying time. I always wash my hair after an outdoor shoot. I had to force myself to get a drink instead of coming over here and touch you. *I don't touch men.*"

He gave her a look.

She grimaced. "You know what I mean. Indiscriminately." She let out an angry sigh. "It's bad enough to feel like this…so out of control, without facing the fact while the attraction might be mutual, it's not necessarily at the same level."

He said a pithy Chinese curse, knowing she wouldn't know what it meant. Why did women have to analyze things like this? Emotions…as if they were something logical to be measured and compared. Desire was desire. He felt it. She felt it. They both struggled with control. Did it matter if he was better at winning the battle? Should he not be? He was the man, a man moreover who was used to being in control of more than his own life.

He'd been here with his mother and sisters, though. Seen them do the same thing with other men, with him even over different things. It frustrated the hell out of him, but he also knew he had to answer her concerns or the problem would only escalate. He had seen that, too.

He brushed her hair behind her ear, a deliberate gesture of affection that connected them. "I did not say I did not feel this inexplicable draw, merely that my choice to follow it was my own. As is yours, *carida*."

"I'm not sure I'm making choices I would otherwise do."

He was careful not to let the exasperated sigh trapped in his chest escape. Of course the choices were unique. The situation was different than anything he'd experienced and he was sure it was the same for her. "I would not have minded if you came over and touched me, but the fact that you did not shows that you have easily as strong a sense of control as I do." Or at least very close to it. "What we feel *is* mutual. So, too, is our unwillingness to let it completely control us."

She looked so damn uncertain and that was not an expression he wanted to see on her face. She needed a more concrete connection than a small touch of affection. She needed to feel his desire and know it was as real as her own. He took her water from her and placed it on the small table; then he tugged her from her chair straight into his lap.

She gasped, her aqua eyes going wide. "What are you doing?"

"Shoring up your confidence." As his head

lowered toward hers, he assured himself this was for her, not his overactive libido.

Their mouths touched and all thoughts of altruism fled while electricity sparked and crackled between them. Never had such a simple, almost chaste caress caused such a conflagration to his senses. Rapacious hunger blazed to life inside him for more of the tempting lips that tasted like the best sex he had ever had, but as sweet as vanilla spice.

Her mouth fit his perfectly and he explored every millimeter of her soft flesh, memorizing her taste and feel on an elemental level he did not begin to understand. He felt like Adam discovering the delights of Eve, but he was no inexperienced youth. He had known many women sexually and yet he could not deny the sensation of newness coursing through him now. It made no sense and his superior brain was too hazy with desire to attempt to understand.

Compulsively he ate at her lips, every nip, lick and caress making him crave more. *He could not get enough.* He wanted more…to go deeper, to claim all that she would give him. He pulled her lower lip between his teeth and sucked demandingly. She took the hint and opened her mouth for him with a small, high-pitched moan.

His big body shuddered under her and he plunged inside with his tongue, tightening his hold on her, yanking her body to press against his. Soft to hard. Curves to muscular contours. Perfect complements, all the more arousing for how right it felt. She was stiff for a heartbeat, as if she would try to hold herself back, but then she melted into him, her arms sliding around his neck.

Damn. Nothing had ever felt this good and he was not even inside of her. She fit him as if they'd been created for this very connection…it would be even better when they made love. It would be perfection.

Her tongue tangled with his, sliding and sparring in perfect feminine counterpoint to his masculine aggression. Her taste intoxicated him more effectively than a magnum of his favorite champagne and his head swam. He wrapped his hand in her hair, holding her head in place, though she was making no effort to move it. He had to taste every hidden recess of her mouth and mark it with his taste as his own.

He'd never felt this primitive possessiveness before, but it felt right, too.

Too damn right.

The frisson of alarm from that thought did not stop him from increasing the carnality of the kiss.

He cupped her hip, sliding his hand in a caress along her leg, his thumb dipping down to brush her inner thigh through her skirt. She trembled, her slim legs parting slightly in tentative invitation. She was so thin, she felt like a waif in his arms. A very sexy waif, but with an ephemeral quality that engendered the irrational fear she would float away.

His hold on her hair tightened involuntarily, but even in his aroused state, he was careful not to pull at the silky strands. This woman would feel nothing but pleasure at his hand. Ever. Or anyone else's, his predator's mind growled in unexpected warning as his other hand slid around to cup her bottom possessively.

She moaned at his hand's movement on her beautifully shaped derriere. The silky fabric of her dress acted as no barrier to his touch. He could feel the heat of her smooth skin beneath it and explored each dip and valley of her bottom before returning to her thighs where he moved inexorably toward her delta.

She cried out against his mouth when his fingers brushed against her apex and she arched her pelvis in blatant invitation. His sex was so hard, it pressed against confinement. He surged up from the chair, molding her body to his and using his hold on her backside to move her against his erection. He'd never been so close to spending in his trousers.

He rocked their bodies together, seeking some measure of relief for the agonizing pleasure. He wanted her. Now.

He considered dropping to the floor and having her right there, but a final spark of sanity prevailed and he headed toward the bedroom with her body locked against his. She didn't seem to notice their movement, writhing in his arms, kissing him ferociously.

But when he pressed her back onto the bed and came down on top of her, she tore her mouth from his. "Wait! What are we doing?" The words came out between gasps that made his male pride spike.

"Do not tell me you do not know, *mi dolce carida.*" Oh, she *was* sweet and utterly delicious.

Particularly the way she bit her bottom lip,

her aqua eyes almost pleading with him. "I thought we were going to have dinner."

She could not be serious. They were practically making love with their clothes on. "I would rather have you." He emphasized the point by thrusting against her with his hardness.

Instead of renewed pleasure, alarm flared in her eyes. "Not now...not yet...*please, Miguel*."

His body screamed at him to convince her otherwise. He could tell it would not take much, but her expression—marked both with trust and vulnerability—demanded he protect her....even from himself.

He rolled onto his back and then stood from the bed in a jerky movement, far from his usual smooth control. "Dinner it is."

He put his hand out to help her up and then thought better of it and dropped it to his side. "I will leave you to refresh yourself."

She sat up, looking dazed and a bit wobbly herself. "Thank you."

"I *will* have you, Amber."

"I believe you." She sounded so fervent, so sincere.

A laugh choked from him as he turned to

leave. He would have her, but it was going to be an adventure getting there.

Amber sat on the bed for several seconds before she managed to stand and make her way to the bathroom to put her hair and makeup back in order.

What had just happened?

She'd been inches away from making love to him. A few more minutes of those self-control stealing kisses and she would have forgotten the words *no* and *wait* even existed. In fact, if the sensation of having a man on top of her wasn't so incredibly alien, she wouldn't have remembered them at all.

No doubt about it. If he had pushed it, she would have given in. But he hadn't. The part of her heart that had been melting since his first smile gushed warmth through her. He'd respected her need to wait and that was every bit as tantalizing and seductive as his kisses had been.

She wrapped her arms around her middle and hugged herself, a goofy smile that would never grace the cover of a magazine playing on her lips. She could definitely fall in love with this man.

Despite the earthshaking nature of the kiss, it actually took very little to get herself looking presentable again. She was definitely more shattered on the inside than showed on the outside. Though her eyes looked somewhat shell-shocked and she really didn't mind him seeing that.

He hadn't looked exactly unaffected when he'd left the room, either.

He was drinking something from the minibar when she came back into the main room. She detected the pungent fragrance of whiskey and appreciated the further evidence of how strongly their intense kissing had affected him.

He turned to face her, his gaze traveling over her like seeking hands. "Ready?"

"Ye…" She had to clear her throat and try again. "Yes."

His hold on the glass tightened until his knuckles showed white, and then he finished his drink in one swallow, before putting the glass down. "Let us go."

He was silent on the walk to the elevator, and during the ride to the lobby. He didn't take her arm when they exited it, either, but led her outside without so much as looking back to see if she followed. He gave his claim ticket to the parking valet and they both waited without speaking for the car to arrive. Once it did, he allowed the parking attendant to open her door while he went around to get in the driver's side.

The silence shimmered with tension and she didn't know what to do to break it. Was he angry with her for calling a halt to the lovemaking? He hadn't acted as if he was at the time, but his lack of communication now made her feel an unaccustomed nervousness. No wonder she'd avoided relationships in favor of her career. The man-woman thing wasn't easy.

He pulled into traffic while she wondered what to say. Finally she decided on straight-forward honesty. "Miguel?"

"Yes, *carida?*"

"Are you angry with me…for stopping us?"

"No. We have met only today, no matter how strong the attraction, I would have to be a real bastard to expect you to accept me into your body so quickly."

"You've never had sex with a woman you just met?"

"Not a woman like you."

"I'm special then?"

"I thought we had already established that."

"It doesn't hurt to reiterate things like that for a woman."

"I will keep that in mind."

"Do that."

"Make no mistake, I want you."

"I know."

"And you want me."

"Very much, but I'm not like that."

"You would have regretted making love. I figured that out."

"Smart man."

"When we make love, I will leave you no room for regret."

She hoped that was true. "So, you are definitely not angry?" she felt the need to confirm.

"No."

"You've been silent. Since I came out of the bedroom, I mean."

"Control does not always come without a cost."

"What do you mean?"

"Concentration. It has taken much concerted effort not to attempt to change your mind."

"I really appreciate the fact that you haven't."

"I am glad. It is worth the cost then."

"I truly think it is," she hastened to assure him.

He smiled and she felt like she'd landed the cover of *Vogue*. "You charm me, Amber Taylor."

"You entrance me, Miguel Menendez."

"Ah…I like to hear this."

"I like being able to say it."

He laughed. "You are very forthright."

"Does that bother you?"

"No. I like it. There are no games between us."

"I don't like emotional games." She'd never played them, but even in business people tried and they annoyed her to no end.

"We have this in common also."

She grinned and looked out the window, her eyes hungry for a bigger glimpse of Barcelona than she'd had so far. She loved the way the city seemed to be a confusing mixture of Gothic, modern and postmodern architecture. The confusion had a charm all its own and she looked forward to walking the streets to soak it in.

"So, where are we going for dinner?" she asked, hoping it would require a drive across the city so she could see more than she had between her hotel and the modeling shoot site.

"My home."

Her heart contracted and then started beating ultrafast. "But…"

"I will not seduce you tonight, Amber. You have said that you must be up very early for your shoot tomorrow. When I do take you to my bed, it will be for hours on end. Such a night would not work for you this evening."

"Thank you for realizing that." But she couldn't help shivering at the implication of his words. *Hours on end?*

CHAPTER FOUR

"WHAT time will you be finished tomorrow?"

"I can never be sure, but if it goes like today, the photos they want should be taken by midmorning."

"And then the job, it is over, is it not?"

"Yes."

"I will pick you up for lunch from your hotel room and we will celebrate a successful shoot."

"Is that what we're going to do?"

"Yes," he said, totally missing or ignoring her gentle sarcasm. "Be prepared to spend the rest of the day and evening with me. I will arrange my schedule."

The man was just a tad too confident. "And *my* schedule?"

"You will be finished with your work you said."

"Perhaps I planned to take a tour of the city

later in the afternoon." Which is exactly what she had planned to do.

"Anything you want to see, I will show you."

"Really?" This could be interesting.

"Yes."

"Because you know, I planned to buy a Bus Turistic ticket and go to every stop on the city's sponsored tourist route."

He laughed. "You are ambitious."

"I have a week for sightseeing."

"Perhaps you will allow me to be your guide…and maybe you will even consent to stay in my fair city longer than a week."

She had only a couple of very minor jobs lined up for the week after her official vacation and for the first time ever, she considered canceling them to play. Shock at her own thoughts kept her speechless for several seconds before she choked out, "I'll consider it."

"I assure you, I will make a better tour guide than those found on the bus. I am native Catalan after all."

"And that makes you superior?"

"Of a certainty."

She laughed. "I suppose I should give you the chance to prove yourself…" She paused for a long moment. "Or fall on your face."

"The only thing I plan to fall on is you, *cielo*."

"What does that mean?"

"It is Catalan for sweetheart."

"I thought all Spanish noblemen were Castilian."

"I am not of the nobility. My family is as old as any in Spain, but we are Catalan."

"Are you one of the ones who still hopes that Catalonia will one day be an independent nation?"

"All Catalans dream, but I am content with my circumstances."

"Considering what those circumstances are, I'd think you should be."

"It is as difficult to be rich as to be poor."

"Tell that to me when you're having a hard time paying the rent and you've lost your car because you couldn't make the payments."

He spared her a sideways glance. "You have never been in such a circumstance."

"No, I haven't, but I can't help thinking about people who have."

"You are a bleeding heart."

"Better it bleed than to be made of stone."

"On this, I think I can agree. Menendez Industries gives more charitable contributions in dollar amounts and as a percentage of net income than any other privately held company in my country."

"Oh, that's really wonderful." The man was too perfect for her own good. She was falling hard and fast.

She suddenly had a deep desire to call her mom for a little womanly advice and mother-daughter encouragement.

Unaware of the panic flowing through her, Miguel said, "It is imperative to manage our resources both effectively and with a certain amount of compassion for those less fortunate."

"I would not have guessed you would take that stand." But the fact he did impressed her to death.

"So, you learn something the business journals do not tell."

"Why don't they?"

"To make such a thing an object of public propaganda diminishes the thought behind doing it. My family is private about many things, *pequeña*."

"I know what that means and I'm hardly little."

"You are taller than the average woman, yes, but hardly a giant and your figure is so tiny a strong wind would tumble you."

"Hardly."

"It is true."

She bit her lip. Did her thinness bother him? Did he find it unappealing? Then she reminded herself of his reaction to their kissing and shoved the doubts away. "A model has to be thin. The camera can be cruel."

"I had heard this was so, but your body is not merely thin, it is very toned. As close to perfect as it is possible to get without plastic surgery I think."

"Is that a compliment?" She never felt this uncertainty around men, particularly when it came to her looks. They were something she worked hard for and took for granted in the process.

But everything with him was different.

"Definitely."

"Then thank you. I put a lot of effort into staying in shape."

"It shows."

She'd had many other people make similar comments, particularly those in the industry, but never had it impacted her so strongly. She felt caressed by the words spoken in his beautiful, deep voice. They also made her feel beautiful and she realized she could not remember the last time she'd felt that way deep inside.

Not just been aware of her outward beauty as a tool for career's ambitions, not like a stunning model in strong demand, but actually felt like a *beautiful woman*. She liked the feeling. A lot.

Miguel's home turned out to be a penthouse apartment in an exclusive area on the outskirts of the city. So, she'd gotten her wish and had a wonderful look at Barcelona while they drove. They talked the whole time, mostly about her work, which made her feel like he really appreciated who she was, not just what she looked like. And the city, which she enjoyed immensely. He truly was as knowledgeable as any tour guide.

When they reached his apartment, he informed her that the housekeeper who greeted them did not live on premises and would be leaving before dinner. "She's prepared our meal, but we will be serving ourselves."

"That works for me," she said as she looked around her.

The apartment had obviously been decorated

by a professional, but it had Miguel's personality clearly stamped on it. And his wealth.

He smiled. "I thought it might."

Dinner...the whole evening was wonderful. They talked more—about everything from business to family. Miguel's parents played a strong role in his life just as Amber's mother did hers. He obviously loved them and that increased her respect for him. As the evening progressed, she found herself liking him more and more.

And when he took her home early as promised, her opinion of him was in the stratosphere. Maybe even beyond. He could have pushed for intimacy, but by not doing so, he showed his respect for her and his desire to pursue a real relationship, not just sexual fulfillment.

Miguel smiled as he drove back to his home after dropping Amber at her hotel. She was an incredible woman.

He regretted the fact they would have so little time together before he had to fly to Prague. This was a woman he could see spending a great deal of time with for weeks, maybe even months before the initial attraction began to wear. It was a strange feeling and he wished he'd met her earlier, but he was not about to allow regrets to lay a pall over his current enjoyment of her company.

He doubted she expected their association to last beyond her trip to Spain, certainly not more than in a casual sense anyway. Neither of them was in a place to enter a committed relationship. It might be selfish of him, but he did not want to dampen the pleasure by talking about their future parting so early on. The right time would come for such a discussion, but before they had even made it to bed was not it.

Amber stacked the tourist brochures she planned to show to Miguel in a pile in the center of the small table in her suite's living area. The shoot had taken even less time than she had anticipated and she'd had plenty of opportunity to plan her campaign for the day. Miguel had offered to be her tour guide and she was going to take him up on it.

He had not shown up at her shoot today, not that she had expected him to. If he was going to take the rest of the day off to spend it with her, she was sure a man of his responsibilities would have quite a bit to do to make that happen. It made her feel special that he wanted to.

Even so, she wasn't ready to fall into bed with him. Not mentally anyway. Her body was another story and if they went back to his apartment or stayed in her hotel suite even briefly, in bed with him was exactly where they were going to end up.

She wanted to see Barcelona, but even more than that, she wanted to get to know Miguel better before taking the irrevocable step of allowing him into her body. She knew that for her, such a step would be life altering.

She wished she could call her mom, but it was still the middle of the night in California. She considered going down to the hotel's business center and sending an e-mail. She glanced at her watch. Making a quick mental calculation, she decided she had just enough time.

She grabbed the brochures, tucked them into the large over the shoulder bag she'd prepared earlier with things she thought she might need for a day spent with Miguel...and possibly a night. While she wasn't mentally prepared to fall into his bed, she didn't try to fool herself into thinking that there was no possibility of that happening. If he kissed her again like he had last night, there was no saying she'd have the wherewithal to call a halt a second time. So, she'd decided to be prepared for the eventuality rather than blind-sided by it.

But she would put it off with sightseeing for as long as possible.

Sitting down at the computer, she made another decision and when she logged onto her e-mail, she sent a message to her agent first. It canceled her upcoming jobs and extended her vacation for an additional week with the promise that she would be back in Southern California for the major trunk show she'd agreed to participate in.

The e-mail to her mom took very little time to write. Amber simply wrote that she thought she might have found "the one" and planned to spend the day with him, getting to know him better. She also told her mom about the change in her travel plans. She thought the fact she was elongating her vacation by a week and canceling two jobs for the first time ever spoke loudly about the seriousness of her feelings. Her mom would get the message.

When Amber finished with her e-mails, she went outside to wait for Miguel. There was no reason to have him park his car if they were going to go sightseeing. Besides, if he did…the temptation to take him upstairs to her room would be too great.

An expensive-looking sedan with darkly tinted windows pulled up in front of where she stood. She stepped back, not wanting to be in the way of the occupants when they got out.

The rear door near her opened and Miguel stepped out, smiling. "You are waiting eagerly for me, I see."

Her eyes drank him in. His tall, muscular body was encased in a tailored suit he wore as comfortably as he had the more casual clothes he'd had on the day before.

"I thought it would be silly for you to have your car parked if we were going to leave right away again."

"We were thinking alike then. I brought a driver for similar reasons. He will make our excursions much easier to navigate."

"I'm sure he will." But she looked dubiously at the car, though. Somehow the thought of having a driver in the car with them made her feel skittish.

His dark brow quirked. "You are not used to this kind of transport, are you?"

"No. My career is not quite to the point where I get picked up for shoots by a car and driver. I still take a lot of taxis and public transport." Deciding to enjoy it rather than be intimidated by the situation, she grinned.

He swooped, kissing her still smiling mouth with firm possession before lifting his head, his hands cupping her shoulders warmly. "You will do me the favor of not partaking of public transport while you are in Barcelona."

She shrugged, making no promises. She did not know how much time he would be able to give her and she was not going to sit in her hotel room twiddling her thumbs while she could be out seeing the sites.

His eyes narrowed as he helped her into the car. "I will put a car and driver at your disposal when I am not with you."

"That's not necessary, Miguel. I'm quite used to riding public transport."

He slid in to sit beside her on the black leather upholstery. "You will allow me to provide this for you as a favor to me."

"I will?" she asked, crossing her arms and staring at him.

"Do you want me to worry about you when I should be concentrating on business?"

"Of course not." But she didn't mind knowing that he would.

"Then you will avail yourself of my car and driver."

"That's manipulative."

He shrugged, looking supremely unrepentant.

She laughed. "You're very stubborn, but I can be, too."

"But please, not on this issue."

"It really worries you?"

"Yes, *mi cielo,* it does."

She supposed women in his world did not ride the bus. "Fine. If you really want to put a car and driver at my disposal, who am I to turn it down?"

"Exactly." He brushed her cheek. "You are so beautiful, but you hear this all the time, no?"

"It's different coming from you," she admitted.

"I am glad. So, do you have a list of places you want to visit?"

"Yes, I brought the tourist brochures with

me." She turned and dug them out from her oversize tapestry bag, brandishing them with a flourish. "I came prepared."

"Good." He smiled and reached for the glossy advertisements. "We have time to look through these now. It will take more than a few minutes to reach our destination in midday traffic."

"Where are we going for lunch?"

"I thought you might like to eat in a café in the *Barri Gotic*. It is interestingly gothic in that area and very near *La Rambla*."

"Oh, *La Rambla* is on my 'must see' list."

"As it should be. To walk *La Rambla* is to experience a slice of the true heart of Barcelona."

"I also hoped to see some examples of Antoni Gaudi's work."

"The architect's designs are worth seeing to be sure. Tomorrow, I will take you to *Parc Guell*. The snake bench is something to behold, but I think today we will concentrate on our Gothic city center and *La Rambla*. Tonight, I would like to take you to the casino."

"That sounds wonderful." She loved the evidence that he took seriously his self-appointed job of showing her Barcelona.

"I have taken tomorrow to dedicate to you

completely as well as the weekend, but Monday I will have to work."

"Wow."

"Wow?"

"That you would clear your schedule for me."

"Our time together is limited. I wish to make the most of it."

Warmth spread through her. "Now is probably a good time to tell you that I canceled a couple of minor shoots so I could extend my stay in Barcelona by a week."

Pleased satisfaction flared in his gray gaze. "I am very glad."

"Me, too." He'd rearranged his schedule for her and that made her feel pretty good about having done the same for him.

The café he chose for their lunch had opted to decorate with the Gothic theme so strong in the architecture of *Barri Gotic*. The chairs of intricately carved dark wood with red velvet cushions could have been created in the Middle Ages. Their table had small lions heads carved into the four corners of the heavy mahogany stained top and gargoyles on the legs. But the menu was very modern.

She knew better than to dwell on the delicacies offered, though. She ordered a dry salad with a grilled chicken breast and her favorite mineral fizzy water to drink.

Miguel's brows rose over her order. "You do not want to try the local food?"

"I can't afford to."

"In what way?"

"I have to maintain a strict caloric intake to keep my figure in top condition."

"Surely you can indulge once in a while."

"I do, but I choose those indulgences carefully." She smiled. "I learned a long time ago to enjoy things besides the food itself when eating out. For me, it is fuel for my body, to be measured and taken in at the appropriate time."

"What *do* you enjoy?"

"The ambiance of this restaurant. I'm indulging in it, reveling actually. I love the colors and textures. They are a feast for my eyes. My stomach doesn't need one. The company. I am happy to be here with you. Watching other people is usually a favorite pastime of mine."

"I've known many women who watched their figure, but none who saw food in quite the light you do. They always seem to regret what they think they cannot have."

She'd noticed that, too, early on in her career and refused to fall into the trap where food or the desire for it became a controlling element in her life. "That would be a waste of time. I'm much better off adjusting to a limited diet and removing the possible damage to my career a fascination with food could do to it."

He looked at her with something like awe. "You really are stubborn."

"I told you I was."

Reaching across the table, he caressed the back of her hand. "You're also very smart."

"Thank you."

There was nothing overtly sensual about the way he was touching her and yet she felt it on a very intimate level. He might as well have been touching her breast for the way her body responded to the small caress.

She had never considered herself a sexual being. In fact, if someone had asked her before meeting Miguel, she would have told them she thought she was probably frigid. She'd never wanted the things she wanted with him, never responded to blatantly sensual touches the way she reacted to the most innocent caress from his hands.

He cupped her hand, playing his middle finger over her palm while his thumb brushed back and forth over the top of her hand. "Your skin is so soft."

"Is that why you touch me so much?" she asked, trying very hard to control her breathing. This touch didn't feel nearly so innocent. In fact, she felt the caress against her palm all the way to her feminine core.

"It is part of it."

"What is the other part?"

"I want you. I will not have you…yet…so I assuage the ache—partially—with touch."

"You ache?"

"Do you not?"

"But you didn't push last night and today…um… today, you came prepared to take me directly to lunch." Was her palm an erogenous zone?

It had to be, but why had no one ever warned her before. During her "sex talks" with her mother, the issues of palms had never come up. Tongues yes, thighs…and of course breasts, but never palms.

That insidious touch continued while his eyes caressed her with equal intimacy. "As I'm sure you know, anticipation heightens the pleasure so that the wait is more than worth the eventual outcome."

"You're putting off making love on purpose?" she asked, breathless and a little confused.

She'd heard allusions to that sort of thing, but hadn't expected to employ the technique herself. She wasn't the most patient of people and would not have pegged him for being altogether patient, either.

"Aren't you?"

Wow. He thought she was playing sophisticated sex games? If only he knew. "I want to get to know you better. Really, that's all."

"I respect that, but I do not deny the extra benefits of the wait, either."

"I…"

"You are lost for words." He smiled. "That is charming."

"It is?" She thought it was rather gauche.

"Yes, to have you respond so innocently when you are in truth very sophisticated is intensely alluring, but I suspect you are aware of that."

"Um…no…not really. I'm not sure I am as sophisticated as you seem to think I am."

"The world you work in does not leave innocence intact very long."

"Not on an intellectual level, no it doesn't, but there are other kinds of innocence. I am not very experienced personally…with men." She didn't really like admitting it, but felt compelled to do so.

He looked at her for a long moment. "You know, I believe you. I find that more attractive than I would have suspected."

"You do?"

"Yes."

"And that surprises you?"

"I do not make it a habit to date women who are inexperienced. There are too many opportunities for misunderstandings in such a liaison."

"But we are different." He'd said so yesterday.

"Yes, many things about our association are different for me."

The pleasure arcing from her palm up her arm and down to the center of her femininity was making it hard for her to think. "You're lethal, you know that, don't you?"

"I would be very disappointed if you saw me any other way."

She husked out a laugh, but what she really wanted to do was call the car back and attack his body in the back seat. It was a very good thing they'd left the hotel. A very good thing. Pure self-preservation had her jerking her hand from his and putting it out of harm's way in her lap. Or *temptation's* way, at any rate.

The rest of lunch was a study in self-control for her. She had to try to hold up her end of the conversation while watching the way Miguel's lips moved as he spoke sparked fantasies that made her throb in embarrassing places. Usually a people watcher, she found her attention so focused on Miguel, she could not have said if there were any other patrons in the restaurant, or not. Though she was sure there had to be.

She kept forgetting to eat, more interested in observing the play of soft light over his aquiline features. Especially entrancing was the way his body moved when he talked with his hands or laughed.

"If you do not stop looking at me like that, we are not going to make it to the *La Rambla* this afternoon."

CHAPTER FIVE

SHE could feel herself blushing, but she gave up on the embarrassment because she simply couldn't help herself. "Are the shops open during siesta?"

"Not all, but siesta does not start for more than an hour."

"Oh." She looked down to where one of his hands rested on the table. Would he react to her caressing his palm as intensely as she had done to his touch? Her fingers itched to find out.

He abruptly stood. "Let us go."

She let him lead her out of the café, his arm around her waist to guide her. The hold pulled her body close to his and she didn't know about his peace of mind, but it wasn't doing a thing for hers. Or her ability to control the desires raging through her.

The noise and sights of the *La Rambla* offered a small measure of relief. Businessmen dressed much like Miguel walked amidst elderly women, teenagers and obvious tourists. It was a people Mecca, showing the cross section of Barcelona that Miguel had promised. The bird market was filled with a cacophony of sounds; birds chittering, twirping, singing and cawing while sellers hawked their wares and customers bargained for the best prices.

The human sculptures fascinated her and she insisted on stopping at each one they passed to toss a coin, just to see the person who had done such an incredible job of holding their statuesque pose move to a new one.

Miguel bought her flowers at one of the stalls and she clutched them with pleasure while they wandered down the long pedestrian way. When shops started closing, he took her to a café for a drink and then on a short walking tour of where they'd started earlier in the *Barri Gotic*. It was very quiet compared to *La Rambla*, but she didn't know if that was because it was the hour of siesta or because it was always that way in central downtown.

"It's deliciously shady down here," she mused, *almost* used to the way it felt to have his arm around her waist.

"The buildings are close. There are many areas that have not seen direct sunlight in more than a century, sometimes far longer."

"Wow. I remember being in New York City once and walking down a narrow road between skyscrapers. I wondered then if the sun ever shone on the pavement."

"Most likely not, *pequeña,* but when it is hot, that is not a bad thing."

"No." She inhaled the air that seemed to carry the fragrance of the age of the city's inner center. "It's relaxing here."

"I think so, though I do not come here often enough. My offices are in a newer part of the city."

She understood that. "I think it's easy to take the beauty of our home for granted. I can go weeks without visiting the beach."

"Do you live near it?"

"Yes, it's less than a fifteen-minute walk from our house."

"Our?"

"I live with my mother. I've never seen any reason to move out and she's happy to have me there. My career takes me away so often, it just seemed a waste to get my own apartment."

"Perhaps this explains your lack of experience with men as well."

"I suppose so." She didn't see any need to reiterate the fact that she'd never felt this way with another man. If she had, she didn't think living with her mother would have stopped her from having a relationship. The truth was, Helen Taylor had suggested more than once that Amber needed to date more.

"Shall we go back to my apartment for the rest of siesta?"

Amber did not think they would be leaving it again that night if they did, but she realized she was ready for that. More than ready. At least physically and right now, her desires were waging an effective battle with her common sense.

"If that is what you want."

He turned her to face him and met her eyes in the shadowy light of the narrow cobbled street. "The question, *mi cielo,* is whether that is what you want. I can return you to your hotel suite and come for you later to take you to the casino."

Part of her wished he would kiss her and take the decision out of her hands, but a much bigger part really liked the way he refused to push her. If all he wanted from her was sex, wouldn't he be a lot more insistent on getting it? There was no doubt that he wanted her, not with the hungry way his eyes devoured her or the way he was constantly touching her.

She licked her lips, a nervous habit she'd thought she'd broken as a teenager. It dried her lips and messed up lip makeup for a shoot. "I want to do both…go back to the safety of my hotel for a while and join you at your penthouse for the siesta…and more."

He cupped her face, his thumbs brushing along the underside of her jaw. "The question is, which do you want more?"

"Shouldn't it be which one is better for me?"

"There is no danger in my arms, Amber."

There was…to her heart. But that danger was in the air around her since she'd met him, too. Not merely in his arms.

"Kiss me."

"If I do, you know you will end up at my apartment."

"I know," she whispered, her head dipping so their eye contact broke.

He tipped her head back, refusing to allow her to look away. "Knowing that, you want my kiss?"

She nodded, incapable of explaining. But it felt right, to seal this thing between them here in the oldest part of the city that beat with the heart of the Catalan, with his heart. It might be reckless. It might even be foolish. But if she did not take this chance, she would always wish she had, of that she was absolutely sure.

His mouth came down, his lips brushing hers gently. Her eyes slid shut and her senses diminished to the hushed sounds of siesta in the city's center and the fragrance of warm summer air mixed with old buildings. Then finally to the feel of his mouth on hers, exploring and tantalizing with each tiny movement.

She had expected a sensual onslaught, but what she got was a promise. The first bud of spring, the kiss of the summer sun on the pale skin of winter, a scarlet leaf floating to the ground to be the first in the splendorous autumn carpet, the first snowflake to fall on Christmas Eve.

She did not know how long the kiss lasted, but when he lifted his head, she felt claimed with a promise of pleasure that was so much more than sexual gratification.

She swayed against him and he tucked her

into his side while flipping out his cell phone to call his chauffeur.

Her cell phone rang when they were in the car on the way to his penthouse. She dug it from her bag and noted the caller. "It's my mom, I need to take it."

Miguel nodded. "By all means."

He had made no move to kiss her again once they had gotten in the car, but sensual energy shimmered between them, the tension so thick it should have made the air hazy.

Hoping none of that would show in her voice, Amber flipped the phone open and put it to her ear. "Hello, Mom."

"Hey, sweetie…what's this about meeting the man of your dreams?"

She was glad her mom's voice wasn't the kind to carry, but she turned a little away from Miguel anyway, switching the phone to her ear farthest from him. "I'll tell you all about it later, Mom."

She saw from the corner of his eye that he pulled his phone out and had started speaking quietly into it.

"Are you with him now?" Her mom was quick.

"Yes."

"That's wonderful, honey. What's his name?"

"Miguel."

"Miguel…" Her mom paused for a count of two. "Do you mean Miguel Menendez?" she asked, sounding shocked and maybe a little worried.

"Yes."

"According to what I know of him, he's never had a long-term relationship."

"Neither have I."

"He dates a lot more than you do, sweetheart." Yes, definitely worried. And her mom hadn't read that in the business journals, or maybe she had. Innuendo was not reserved for the tabloids only.

"It's okay, Mom. Trust me."

"I'm glad you're noticing a man, don't get me wrong. For a while, I wondered if you were honest-to-goodness married to your career. But Miguel Menendez?"

"Yes." That was all she said. She couldn't say more, not in front of Miguel, and that would be too embarrassing. But she and her mom understood each other.

"You can't always choose where your heart leads you."

"Exactly."

"He must be pretty special to have broken through your wall of indifference to men."

"Definitely."

"I'm glad, sweetie. Really glad." That was her mom, always supportive—even when she was a little apprehensive.

"Thanks, Mom. Talk to you later?"

"Sounds good. Have fun!"

"Love you, Mom."

"Love you, too, Amber. So much."

They hung up, Amber smiling.

"You two are very close."

"Yes, since my dad died before my birth all we've ever had is each other."

"She never remarried?"

"No. She's dated a few times, but she says that no one has ever made her happier than her memories."

"Your parents must have had a very good marriage."

"According to her, it was the best. Worth keeping a memory intact over."

"Your mother is a remarkable woman."

"She is. She wasn't sure about my modeling at first. She tried to talk me out of it, and then one day she came to me and said

I should pursue my dreams no matter what they were. And there's been no looking back since. But I've always been determined to prove to her that she didn't make a mistake supporting me in my dreams."

"That is laudable."

"Is laudable sexy?"

"On you, *cielo,* everything is sexy."

"We aren't going to leave your apartment again tonight, are we?" He'd said as much before he kissed her, but it was starting to sink in more firmly exactly what that meant.

"Does the prospect bother you?"

"No. Not much," she added with more candor.

"You have nothing to fear. It will be very good between us."

"Um…" She licked her lips again and then sighed. "I'm sure you are right. Only there's something I think you should know."

"What is that?"

One thing she'd learned long ago, in cases of true importance blunt was better than tap dancing around a subject. "I've never been with another man *that way.*"

He stared at her, looking totally poleaxed. "*¿Que dice?*"

"I told you I wasn't very experienced."

"*Not very* is not the same as *completely without*."

"Well, no it's not. Are you saying you don't want me because I'm a virgin?" She'd never anticipated that, but she should have. He'd already said he normally went for women who knew their way around a bedroom, or at least that's what he'd implied.

"No. I…" His voice trailed off and he stared at her some more, something indefinable flaring in his features. "Why are you a virgin?"

"What do you mean why?"

"Have you been saving yourself for marriage?"

"That's a really archaic concept." Though one she wasn't totally against, but the truth was, it hadn't been anything that defined in her mind. "I've never wanted another man enough to make love, to let him into my life like that."

"I want to make love to you, over and over again. If you want truth, I feel like I cannot breathe for the hunger inside me." He didn't sound particularly happy about that fact, but she understood. It was overwhelming to want someone that much, even for a man like Miguel.

"I want you like that, too."

He nodded. "But we are making no promises for the future."

"Of course not." They'd only known each other a couple of days. No matter how strong the physical attraction or how right it felt when they were together, they didn't know each other well enough to start talking long-term commitments.

Though she knew deep inside that she was in love with this man, she was more able to share her body than that particular piece of knowledge. It was just so unbelievable. The whole love at first sight thing was a myth. It had to be, but she felt something for him that went beyond physical desire and originated in the region of her heart.

Still, she was no more ready to make a lifetime commitment than he was. Probably even less so. Her career was just taking off. It was the worst possible time for her to take a break and pursue personal ambitions. But they had two weeks and who knew what they could work out after that?

His expression reflected unmistakable

relief, quickly followed by sensual hunger. "You do me a great honor, allowing me to be your first lover."

"I don't think I have a choice."

"I know this feeling. I feel it, too. I want to touch you now…to learn your body's secrets."

"But the driver…"

"I could close the privacy window, but that would embarrass you, would it not?"

"Yes."

"I have no desire to embarrass you."

"Good." But she was tempted. She clamped her jaw to keep herself from admitting it.

It seemed to take forever to get to the penthouse, but when they arrived the housekeeper had already left.

"I called from the car phone and asked her to take care of a couple of things before leaving early," Miguel explained.

"While I was chatting with my mom."

"Yes."

He put his hand out. "Come."

After a second's hesitation, she took the proffered hand and allowed him to lead her to the bedroom where a bucket of champagne chilled in a stand beside the bed. That along with two glasses on a nearby table, the turned-down bed and drawn curtains spoke of the "things" he'd asked his housekeeper to attend to before leaving.

The room was cast in intimate shadows from the curtains drawn against the afternoon sun, setting an ambiance every bit as romantic as candlelight.

For a long moment they simply stood and faced one another. The desire had been building between them since the moment they met, but at astronomical rates the past hour and her entire body shook with unfamiliar need.

Miguel noticed her trembling and smoothed his hands down her bare arms. "It is time."

"Yes." She felt no trepidation, though perhaps she should, but there was no room for anything but the craving she knew only he could meet.

Thoughts of what would happen, why she was there, what she was feeling—all of them not quite fully formed—flitted through her head as her body grew more and more shivery with arousal beneath his heavy-lidded appraisal.

Her heart was beating fast and she felt it rushing through her veins, the heady liqueur of arousal heating every cell until she felt the flush of need stealing over her entire body. She could hear her own panting breaths as if magnified by a sound system. They echoed around her while her pulse beat inside her head. Her chest was tight with excitement, but that was nothing compared to the sensation of an electrical charge zapping each of her nerve endings with tiny jolts of life.

That was the right word. Life. She felt so alive with Miguel. Colors were brighter, the air was crisper, smells were more intense. That was why she could distinguish his scent over that of other men. It was calling to her now with an elemental masculinity that defied his sophisticated exterior.

Miguel Menéndez elicited an entire range of emotions in her she had not even thought existed. At least *for her*. Emotions she had never really even wanted and now wondered how she could have been so shortsighted to think she could live without them.

This was glorious. Amazing. *Life*.

He pulled her close with gentle hands, but his face told another story. His expression was feral in its intensity, further proof of the primal male that lurked beneath the tycoon's façade. His dark eyes said his hunger was easily as strong as her own. Perhaps stronger. After all, he knew from *experience* how good this was going to be.

Or did he?

He'd said she was different. Perhaps their intimacy would be unique and special for him as well. She prayed it was so. She needed it to be that way, but the sane bit of her mind that remained told her not to expect it. That kind of wishing was best left for fairy tales where the knights were as innocent as the maidens.

"I will make it perfect for you, *carida*." He spoke with his lips bare centimeters from hers.

"You're so sure you can," she breathed.

"Of a certainty." He made a sexy sound deep in his throat and kissed her, his lips claiming utter possession.

Her knees threatened to buckle and she sagged into him. He took her weight without faltering, looping one arm around her waist and pressing her close. Everything about him was hard and strong and she felt both safe and incredibly sensual molded so perfectly to his body. Running her hands up his sculpted chest under the suit jacket, she kissed him back.

His nipples were rocklike little nubs under the fine fabric of his tailored shirt and he groaned when her fingertips brushed over them. Her own breasts and nipples swelled and ached for his caress. As if reading her mind, his free hand came between them to knead her swollen curves through the light-weight cotton of her black Dolce & Gabbana summer dress.

She hadn't worn a bra because of the spaghetti straps. The lack of additional barrier between his caressing fingers and her sensitized skin increased the intensity of the pleasure. Soon, she was moaning against his lips and pressing herself into him, trying to find a position that assuaged the ache of need growing inside her.

He swept her high against his chest and her arms went of their own volition to loop around his neck. The pulse beating in his neck was as rapid as her own. She savored it with her lips and he stilled in his move toward the bed, his arms convulsing around her. Oooh…she liked that.

She pressed an openmouthed kiss to the underside of his chin, her tongue flicking out to taste him, rasping over the dark stubble just starting to shadow his jaw. He tasted salty and so incredibly masculine.

She kissed along his jaw, nibbling on the hard curve, reveling in his taste and sheer maleness. "You are such a macho man, Miguel."

"I am glad you think so, *cielo*," he rasped, tilting his head so she could reach more of him.

She loved that he was so into her touch and not afraid to show it. His big body shuddered once, like a skyscraper in a low level earthquake, but she never once felt in danger of falling from his strong arms. He really was all man and ultraconfident to boot.

She nipped at his ear and then touched it with her tongue, loving the sound of feral arousal that came from deep in his chest when she did it. Suddenly he was moving again, quickly, across the room, stopping when he reached the oversize bed that dominated the area.

He laid her down with strength leashed by tenderness and stepped back, shrugging his suit jacket off as he moved. His muscles rippled under the form-fitting tailored shirt and she wanted to reach out and touch them. Her arm lifted as if she would, but he was standing too far away.

She watched in avid interest as he stripped

off his clothes with an economy of movement that spoke of impatience and total comfort with his own nudity. She'd seen male models, tons of them in varying states of undress. Had been posed with them in nothing short of intimate situations for the camera, but never had another man's naked or nearly naked body made her own weep.

Moisture pooled in that secret place between her legs and it felt profound. Not merely sexual, but exquisite. Like coming upon a hidden waterfall in the forest—something secret and beautifully lush. To have never experienced the reaction with another man made her body's response all the more special and wildly intimate.

Emotions as well as physical desire swamped her until she felt like she was drowning in a tsunami of need. Silken flesh that had known no man's touch pulsed with agonizing rapacity for his. He stripped off his briefs, his hardness springing free. The flesh was slightly darker than the rest of his skin, stretched taut over an impressively large erection.

For all her exposure to the male body, she'd never actually seen a man in full arousal before. It was both just a little daunting and *incredibly* arousing. Despite the shiver of slight trepidation that skittered down her spine, her untried body instinctively knew what it yearned for and she undulated on the bed in helpless desire.

His eyes darkened until they looked almost black and he stroked himself with a natural sensuality that enhanced the hunger clawing inside her. "You are amazingly sexy, *mi cielo*."

"That is definitely the pot calling the kettle," she said between gasping breaths.

He smiled, his expression filled with promise. "You are by far the most seductive woman I have had the privilege to make love to."

"You're kidding."

"I am not."

"But you've been with tons of women."

"Not exactly tons."

"All of them more experienced than me."

"It is *you* I find so captivating, *mi dolce tesoro*."

His sweet treasure? She shook her head, trying to clear thoughts fuzzy from desire. "I always thought I was sort of sexless," she admitted in a quiet voice.

He looked at her incredulously. "You turn me on so hard it is all I can do not to take you now."

A husky laugh choked out of her throat.

He shook his head. "It is not amusing, trust me on this. I do not want to hurt you and you are innocent."

"Which is why I can't see myself as the most seductive woman you've been with." Yet as unbelievable as it seemed to her, she did not sense he'd said the words out of mere flattery.

"As I said, it is the woman Amber Taylor I find so stimulating, not your level of experience or lack thereof." He climbed onto the bed, one knee beside her hip, the other insinuated between her legs, pushing her skirt indecently high on her thighs. "Though I *am* finding the lack surprisingly tantalizing."

"Oh."

"Do you know what I find difficult to credit?" he asked, leaning over her with his naked body.

"Wh…what?" she asked in an embarrassingly squeaky voice.

"The fact that you have never made love to another man."

"I was never interested." Hence her belief in her own lack of sexual feelings.

"Yet, right now, virgin that you are, you are panting for it."

He was right and the knowledge did not even embarrass her. It was much too amazing. "I guess I was just waiting for the right man."

"And that would be me?" He leaned down and nuzzled her neck, sending chills of pleasure along her neck and shoulders.

"Do you need me to say it?"

CHAPTER SIX

HE KISSED the corner of her mouth. "No, I can see it. And that in itself is an aphrodisiac of unparalleled power."

"Is it?" She licked her lips, tasting him on them.

"Believe it."

"What else excites you?" she dared in a soft voice.

"Everything about you." He kissed her temple. "But specifically?" His lips moved along her cheekbone, tasting her with nibbling kisses the same way she'd explored him earlier. "The way you lay there watching me as if I am the most enticing thing you have ever seen."

"You are."

He groaned and kissed her full on the lips, exploring her mouth with his tongue briefly before lifting his head. "And your honesty...I find that a complete turn-on."

"That's good, because I'm not good at hiding things from you." She'd found herself being shockingly forthright with him from the first words they spoke.

He slid his hand down her thigh, sending her nerve endings rioting. "That surprises me."

"Me, too," she admitted in a voice that hitched on each word as his caresses sent jolts of pleasure zinging through her. "I put on a facade for the camera almost every day of my life…" Her voice trailed off as she turned her head from side to side on the silky pillow.

"But?" he prompted.

"But…from the moment we met, I've found myself blurting out things I would never admit to anyone else."

His hand slid up her thigh until he met the elastic leg of her barely there panties. He skimmed along it with a shiver inducing fingertip. "Good. I do not want you telling another man you want him."

She gasped as he came very close to touching her most private place. "That sounds possessive."

"Count on it. When a woman is with me, she is mine."

"And the converse?"

"As long as we are together, I am yours."

"Then right now, we belong to each other?"

"Yes."

If the moment had felt profound before it now felt as heavy as a megaton barge with meaning. They might not be verbalizing promises, but their bodies were making them for them…the very situation was rife with them.

Not ready to deal with those implications, she asked, "Do you want me to undress?"

He shook his head, his fingertip playing with the edge of her panties. "I prefer to do it."

"Is that part of making this perfect for me?" She barely recognized the husky voice asking the question as her own.

"Yes." He withdrew his hand from her thigh and traced the contours of her face. "Your beauty is such a gift to me."

"You are used to beautiful women."

"You are different. Your beauty goes to your soul, does it not? And I can see that in every luminescent line of your features."

"You make me melt inside when you say things like that."

"I wonder."

"What?" she asked, feeling confused.

"Precisely how melted you are." He winked, switching from romantic seducer to earthy lover in a heartbeat.

She laughed, feeling light with happiness inside. "I don't think we're talking about the same thing."

"Perhaps." Their mouths met briefly. "A man's mind might be a bit more basic than a woman's during times like this."

"Do you think?" Again her voice hitched on each word as his hand moved down her face to her neck, to cup her breast through her dress again.

"More than think, I know." He deftly unbuttoned the tiny white buttons that held her bodice together with one hand. "For instance, all I can think of right now is how your bare breast is going to feel against my palm."

He peeled back her bodice, exposing her intimate curves to both his gaze and the air. The peaks were already beaded in tight points, but she could feel them hardening even more as the temperature controlled air touched them. Then his big hand engulfed her breast, his palm upbraiding the nipple, sending shards of pleasure slicing through her.

She arched toward his hand, sucking in a short gasp of air. "I like that."

He chuckled, the sound dark and sexy. "I do, too, *mi bonita cielo*. But there is something I will like even more."

"What?" she asked on another soft sigh.

"Tasting you." Then his mouth was replacing his hand on her breast and her nipple was sucked into exotic, wet heat.

A keening cry sounded and she vaguely realized it was her as his teeth nibbled the turgid tip. His hand was skimming down her body to her thighs again, not stopping until his fingertip met and delved past the small elastic barrier he'd been playing with before. And then he was touching her where she'd never, ever been touched by another man.

He released her nipple, giving it a sensuous lick before lifting his head to meet her dazed eyes. "You are very nicely melted."

She choked on a laugh, but it was cut off by his lips as he kissed her with heated intensity. He ate at her lips, pressing his tongue into her mouth with demanding eroticism. He knew what he wanted, but she was only too happy to give it to him. The feelings suffusing her body were indescribable...beyond anything she had ever known or even dreamed about.

His mouth devoured hers while he fingered her sweetest flesh, sending pleasure arcing from nerve point to nerve point throughout her body. The kisses the day before had been electrifying to her senses, but these were a full-on hurricane, battering at everything she thought she'd known about herself.

She writhed on the bed, pleasure tension spiraling inside her. She'd touched herself, she knew what an impending orgasm felt like, but this was beyond anything she'd ever felt before. It felt like a storm raged right in the core of her and was getting ready to explode in fury throughout her body. It was terrifying, but absolutely addicting as well.

She could no more break the kiss or push his hand away than she could stop breathing. In fact, stopping breathing would probably be easier.

He adjusted his hand and one blunt male fingertip slipped just inside her slick channel while his heel pressed against her clitoris. At the same time, his tongue thrust into her mouth in a parody of the intimacy he had promised her.

The spiraling pleasure exploded, rocking her body with such intense sensations that she screamed into his mouth. His tongue muffled the sound, but her throat felt raw from it anyway. Showers of sparks detonated inside her while her body convulsed against his restraining one.

His hand kept moving with tormenting pleasure until her body arched and convulsed again so hard that she saw stars, and then went utterly limp. Her eyes closed, her body lax, she floated on a cloud of luscious satiation.

Only then did he pull his hand away and break the kiss. "That was a delicious little appetizer, *mi querida*."

"Ap…appetizer?" she asked, stumbling over the word with her sluggish tongue, her eyes flying open.

His gunmetal gaze glittered with rapacious need. "*Appetizer*. I fully intend for the main event to leave you insensate." He meant it. She could see it in his eyes.

She gasped. "You are ambitious."

"This surprises you?"

"No." But she hadn't realized his competitive nature would stretch into the bedroom, or cause him to want to give her a kind of pleasure that she had no measurable comparison for anyway.

"It is time for me to undress you."

"I'm practically naked already."

"As we have discussed before...practically does not equate to the actuality."

"It will be so different."

"Do you doubt me?"

She shook her head fervently, making him smile.

"Then allow me to continue."

He just smiled as he reached around to unzip her dress and pull it from her unresisting body. Her sandals went next and then his forefingers hooked in the waistband of her tiny panties. "Lift your hips."

"I'll try. I'm still pretty boneless." She concentrated on lifting her pelvis.

"Good girl." He pulled the panties down slowly, caressing her legs with the silky fabric as he went.

She'd been as close to naked as a woman could get in front of the camera, she'd traversed numerous runways wearing little more than a smile and a few scraps of lace or silk, and she'd been completely nude in front of dressers and designers, but she felt like her body was being revealed for the first time. A tidal wave of vulnerability crashed through her.

Would he find her body as beautiful as her face? It was a foolish question. He'd been there yesterday when she'd posed for the camera in a string bikini, but this felt different. Only as she experienced full nudity with him did she appreciate how right he was when he said that *practically* and *actually* were concepts far from one another.

His current silence was not helping to dispel of the fear burgeoning inside her. He knelt there on his knees, simply looking down at her. She thought he might like what he was seeing, certainly there was no visible depreciation of his desire, but his lack of comment grew more unnerving by the second.

"Miguel?"

His gaze did not waver from her body. "Yes?"

"What are you doing?"

"Looking at you."

"Yes, well…I sort of figured that out."

"Have you ever seen a piece of art that stopped you in your tracks, made you stumble as you approached it because of the sheer perfection and beauty of it?"

Was he saying that was how he saw her? "Um…yes…I felt that way the first time I saw a Mary Cassatt in person."

"Her work is amazing, but *mi dolce tesoro*…it is moments like this that mere humanity has to acknowledge the unparalleled artistry of God."

"So…um…you like what you are seeing?"

"Your body is utter perfection."

"My breasts are small."

"Exquisite and perfectly proportioned."

"My bones show in places." It was necessary for the camera, but she felt self-conscious about her thinness for the first time in memory.

He shook his head as if clearing it. "Everything about you is just right. How can you doubt it?" He waved a hand toward his fierce erection. "Is this not ample proof I do not consider you lacking in any physical sense?"

"It's not merely physical, is it?" she asked in a fit of doubt that might be irrational, but was completely unquenchable.

"Have I not told you? The beauty I see begins inside you. You are so much more than a body that is perfectly honed and toned for the life of a model."

"Thank you."

"It is I who should be thanking you for sharing such perfection with me."

"You're no slouch yourself."

His gaze finally met hers. "Do you like looking at me as well?"

"Oh, yes." More than she would have ever thought possible.

And now that he had assuaged her doubts, she felt shivery with pleasure from having his gaze on her as well. She would not have thought such a thing would excite her. To be looked at. But she felt the pleasure building inside again from the intensity of his gaze alone. Well, okay, maybe from the view, too.

He truly was magnificent.

He leaned down to kiss her again. Only his lips landed on the top slope of one petite breast. He did not go directly for her nipple like he'd done before, but explored every centimeter of her swollen curves with his mouth and especially his tongue. He swirled it around first one aureole and then the other, over and over again.

The heat in her core built again to molten levels. "Miguel!"

"What, *mi dolce?* What do you want?"

"You know."

"Say it."

"No." She tried to direct his head so his mouth was over her nipple. "I can't."

But he hovered teasingly above the hard peak, brushing the puckered flesh with the lightest caress.

"Please, Miguel...please..."

"Please, what? Say it, *mi* Amber. I want to hear the words from your mouth."

"Suck it...please...put my nipple in your mouth."

He growled and then did just that.

She screamed as pleasure seized her with harsh force. The few times she had considered what sex might be like, she'd never thought it would be something so primal and earthy. That it would shatter her with pleasure while making her body scream for more. He suckled her while she whimpered with the sheer amazing wonder of it.

Her hands explored the muscular contours of his back while she used the rest of her body to caress what she could reach of his. Her thigh brushed his heated shaft and they both shuddered from the contact. She reached down to touch it. She could only reach the head, but she grasped it with shaking fingers.

He tore his mouth from her breast. "Oh, damn… Amber…stop."

"I want to touch you."

"Next time…but right now, I must keep my control."

"I don't want you controlled."

"I refuse to hurt you, but it would be all too easy to do so because it is your first time." He gently, but inexorably removed her hand from his hardness. "Next time, I promise, *querida*, you may touch me to your heart's content."

"I will hold you to that."

"I look forward to it, but right now…I want to taste you."

Expecting him to do what he'd done the last time he said that, she was totally unprepared for his swift change in his position and the mouth that descended on the apex of her thighs to kiss the top of her mound. She automatically tried to close her thighs, but his shoulders were there.

She grabbed at his hair. "Wait, Miguel…I don't think…"

He lifted his head, the sheer erotic image of his head between her thighs scorching her consciousness. "This is not the time to think, it is the time to feel."

"But…"

"Open your legs all the way for me, I want to see what you have shown no one else."

"You want to see me…there?"

"Yes." His hot gaze burned her. "Very much."

"All right." What else could she say? In that moment, she realized she would deny this man nothing.

Perhaps she should have been embarrassed, but it seemed so natural to move her thighs into a wide V.

He pushed her ankles until her knees bent and she was exposed completely to his gaze.

He smiled a predator's smile. "Very pretty." He touched the flesh still sensitive from his earlier ministrations, brushing along her silky wet, swollen lips. *"Very, very pretty."*

She couldn't think of a thing to say in response to that, so she said nothing.

Eyes darkened by desire met hers. "Now…I am going to taste the essence of you."

Her mouth opened in automatic denial, but he was already bending down to do as he'd promised. Even more intimate than the sweet kiss he'd placed on the top of her moist curls, his tongue tasted her with devastating expertise. The pleasure that had been on a slow build since he started this "looking game" spiked sharply upward until she was moaning and arching into his mouth.

Then she felt one finger delve deeply into her. He hit her barrier and she jerked away at the unexpected pain. But he followed her with his finger, pressing gently against the barrier, but not breaching it. It was uncomfortable, but did not hurt as the initial touch had done. She forced her body to relax. She wanted him inside her...that meant she would have to accustom herself to the touch...to the pressure against her still intact innocence.

He continued to kiss her with his tongue while his finger moved in and out, pressing oh so carefully each time, until she was once again moving into his touch instead of pulling away from it. His thrusts with his hands increased in intensity until, with one sharp jab, he broke through her barrier.

She cried out, but it wasn't just in pain. It hurt, though not terribly, not nearly as bad as she'd heard it could be. But along with the minimal pain was the incredible knowledge that he had just broken through her virginity. She belonged to him and by touching her like this, he had given himself to her.

While they were together.

She dismissed the reminder of his earlier words, but a tiny chill from the implied caveat blew through her heart.

The finger inside of her was still, giving her time to adjust to having him inside her. But he continued to lash her pulsing sweet spot with his tongue, renewing the pleasure diminished by the small sting of deep penetration for the first time. It felt so good, so intense…she had to move, arching and retracting her pelvis back and forth against his hand and mouth, moaning as she did so.

A second finger joined the first as she pressed against him, making her whole body shake violently with want and her moans turned to a keening cry.

He lifted his head. "You are ready for me."

It wasn't a question, so she didn't answer. She couldn't have if she'd needed to, not coherently anyway. She whimpered and her body arched in protest against the loss of his intimate kiss, though.

He pressed his free hand against her belly

as he withdrew his fingers. "Shh…we merely exchange one pleasure for another."

How could he sound so together…so *coherent*…when she felt like she was on the verge of flying apart?

Even those thoughts splintered as he moved up her body and she shivered wildly at the contact of so much naked skin to naked skin. And then he was *there,* where she felt empty and in need—the big, blunt tip of his erection pressing against her swollen, silky wet flesh. His gray gaze held hers with the power of a tractor beam as he rocked forward, penetrating just inside her opening and going no farther.

She jerked and keened again, the sensation so beyond anything she'd ever known she wasn't sure she wouldn't pass out from both the pleasure and the shock of it.

"All right?" he asked, sweat beading on his forehead.

She shook her head and then nodded.

His jaw clenched, but then he gave her a strained smile. "Which is it? Yes or no?"

"O-okay," she forced out in a tiny breath-less gasp. "I th-think I'm okay."

"Only think?"

"Is okay," she said with more conviction than volume. She could barely hear herself.

But he heard her, his eyes glowing with something wild and primitive, as he pushed forward in a steady, careful, but relentless campaign to claim her untried depths. Her body was inexperienced, but he had aroused her to such heights that silky moisture smoothed his way and swollen flesh gave way around him.

Finally he was seated fully inside her, their pelvises touching, his member gently nudging her cervix.

She sucked in a breath and nearly choked on it.

He made a hissing sound. "You are very tight, *querida*."

"I think you're a little big." She was rather proud of the multiple words strung together.

He laughed, the sound rich and seductive…and maybe a tiny bit breathless. "You think we have a logistical problem?"

She felt stretched and filled…and even a little tender, but she had no doubts he was meant to fill her just like this. When she had considered what making love would be like, she'd always thought it would feel just a little alien to have another person inside her, but it didn't…it felt as if she was being completed, not invaded. "No."

"Good. I believe my patience is very near to gone. I am not sure I would have the strength to hold back and reassure you."

She, on the other hand, had no doubts. The man had already proven to have superhuman willpower. If she'd needed him to, he would have soothed her, she was sure of it. But she didn't need that. This was much too *right*.

She opened her thighs a little wider in an invitation both archaic and profound. "I'm fine."

He groaned, arching back and surging forward as if her words had detonated inside him. The slide of intimate skin against intimate skin made her whimper with delight.

He stilled immediately. "Did I hurt you?"

"No," she groaned. "Move…need you to *move*."

The laughter this time was almost diabolical. He moved, though—stroking in and out with deliberate but agonizingly leisurely movements.

"Feels so good," she panted.

He threw his head back, the tanned

column of his neck showing muscles straining. "Yes, it does."

He said something else...she was sure it was in Catalan because it didn't sound either quite French or Spanish. And why that increased her already heart-stopping excitement levels she didn't know, but it did. Oh, goodness, yes it did.

She tilted her pelvis toward his downward movements, trying to increase the friction, needing something more, but not sure what. Miguel didn't react outwardly to her movements, but kept up the long, slow thrusts as if he was intent on her feeling every single centimeter of each purposeful slide.

It was too much, though...or maybe not enough. She'd been so close to the pinnacle of pleasure before that she hovered tensely on its edge now, the incredible intimacy of the act driving higher the tension calling for release inside her.

"Please, Miguel...please...move...I need..."

"*Me.* You need me, *querida.*" He drove inside her with a thrust that made her feel as if he was going to reach her heart from the inside. "Do not forget it."

"Won't. I need you."

He said something else…but this time it sounded like the Chinese cursing he'd been doing the other day. And then he increased his pace until they were making love to a primal drumbeat created by the slap of flesh against flesh.

She'd never known anything so wonderful…or exotic, or powerful…or flat out overwhelming. "Yes! Oh, yes!"

She moved with him with instinctual rhythm that seemed to drive him wild because his hands gripped her hips and he slammed into her with pounding force. A storm of sensation whipped through her, driving her irrevocably toward the peak of a Category 5 Hurricane. But when the cataclysm came this time, she was not alone. She screamed, her entire body arching and convulsing in incomparable joy and he was going rigid in her arms, his hips grinding into hers and her name a primal shout above her.

The pleasure was so intense, tears streamed from her eyes and her lungs lurched on a sob.

His head was still tilted back and he looked like an ancient warrior calling to the heavens in victory.

His body shuddered and jerked and then he

bucked his hips once, twice, three more times…each movement drawing aftershocks of pleasure from both of them until she thought she might die from the surfeit.

"It's too much," she gasped.

He didn't answer, just lowered his head with a growl and swooped down to claim her mouth. It was not a gentle, aftermath salute, but erotically possessive and almost brutal in its intensity. With a stunned thrill, she realized it was exactly what she needed and she responded with a residual passion that shocked her as much as she enjoyed it.

Their bodies moved together, more aftershocks of pleasure pulsing between them until eventually, the kiss calmed and the movements slowed. He finished it with a tender salute to both corners of her mouth and her closed eyes, while their bodies molded together in a oneness that had to be as spiritual as it was physical.

"Amber."

She forced her eyelids to lift. "Mmm?"

"*Gracias*. Thank you."

"You're welcome." Though she didn't know what he was thanking her for. It seemed to her that the pleasure had been satisfyingly mutual.

"You gave me a gift of unequal measure."
He kissed her again, this time oh so gently.

Pleasure filled her. "I didn't think men saw innocence that way anymore."

He smiled ruefully and shook his head. "I am talking about the gift of yourself and your passion. To choose me as your first lover is another honor and one I will always treasure."

And she knew, right then, that she loved him. Completely. Totally. And forever.

He left the bed and it was only as he walked toward the bathroom that she realized he'd thought to use protection. She almost choked on her own irresponsibility. She hadn't even thought about it, not once. But pregnancy was not something she wanted to deal with at this stage in her life.

Honestly, she'd never even considered having children at all. Now that she'd met him, there was a sweetness to the idea she never would have expected. She knew her mom would love to be a grandmother one day, but she'd never pressured Amber to get married and provide babies. Now was definitely not the time, with her career on the brink of great things, but maybe one day it would be.

She heard bathwater running peripherally

to her ruminations, so she was not totally
shocked to be scooped from the bed by a still
very naked Miguel and carried into the large
en suite. But when he lowered them into the
sunken roman style bath together, a frisson of
something akin to shock went through her. It
felt almost as intimate to be bathing with him
as the act of lovemaking.

CHAPTER SEVEN

HE SANK to a bench in the foaming water and settled her on his lap, then proceeded to wash her body with slick glycerin soap scented with the fragrance of honeysuckle.

"This seems like a really girly soap for you to have," she commented.

"I find it is best to be prepared for any eventuality."

"Like feminine guests who stay over?"

"Yes."

Her body went rigid as her mind assimilated the implications. "Oh."

"My mother and sisters make a habit of using my apartment as their base when shopping in the city."

Oh. That was much better than what she'd been thinking. "The family home isn't in convenient driving distance to the city?"

He shrugged. "Not according to them."

"It must cramp your style a bit to have drop-in family guests."

"In what way?"

"Socially."

His eyes lit with understanding and he shrugged again. "I do not bring other women here."

"You don't?"

"No."

"Never?"

"Never."

"Why me?"

"We have already decided you are the exception to the rule."

"Wow."

"And our time together is limited. I did not want to waste precious hours in transit between hotels and my home."

"Wow, again." He was really serious about spending maximum amount of time with her while she was in Spain.

Her newly fledged love surged in a warm wave through her.

"Wow, indeed." He got a really intent, serious look on his face. "You might consider this moving too quickly, but I would like you to consider staying with me for the remainder of your time in Barcelona."

Her jaw dropped. "Seriously?"

"Very much so, but I will understand if you feel I am moving too quickly." The words were right, but the expression in his eyes didn't match.

If she said no, he was going to try to convince her otherwise. Only she had zero intention of saying no. "The truth? Making love for my first time after only meeting you yesterday already has us on what I consider a light speed relationship course."

"Sometimes, we must seize the opportunity when we have it."

"I agree."

"So, you will stay here?"

"Yes." The speed with which their relationship had moved was terrifying and in fact, moving in with him for the two weeks would be more a comfort than an additional burden.

She needed the closeness for reassurance.

"Good." That was all he said, but his whole body radiated satisfaction.

Her lips curved in a smile, though it took almost too much effort. Making love was exhausting. He finished washing her, soothing her with his touch until she was liquid and boneless in his arms...so sleepy she snuggled her head against his shoulder, her eyes sliding closed.

She made no demur when he helped her from the bath and then proceeded to dry her with careful hands and a super soft, plushy towel right off the heated rack. He carried her into the bedroom and tucked them both between the Egyptian cotton sheets. The last thing she remembered as she slid into sleep was the press of his lips against her temple.

Amber woke encased in heat.

Instead of a soft pillow under her head, it rested against short, silky hair covering a muscular chest. A reassuring beat sounded against her ear, its soothing cadence filling her with a sense of well-being. There was no moment of disorientation, no wondering where she was and how she'd gotten there or who was in the bed with her.

She knew exactly where she was and whose strong arm was curved across her back. Which was odd really and she couldn't help taking a second to ponder the strangeness of her reaction if not her circumstances.

She should have been at least a little disoriented in waking up against another person. The only other times she'd ever shared a bed had been when she was sick as a child and her mom had taken Amber into her bed in case she woke feeling worse in the night.

She'd never even fallen asleep against a man's chest while traveling, or so much as dozed on a warm sandy beach close enough to touch another body. And she was used to having the entire expanse of at least a double-size bed to herself, but lying there curled against Miguel's big body felt absolutely right. Not weird. Maybe new, but not something she had to get used to. Just…*right*.

More right than anything she'd ever known actually. And that was disorienting. Very. How could it be so perfect so quickly? How could she feel like she was meant to be exactly where she was even though it wasn't anything she'd anticipated…could ever have anticipated?

And even more than the rightness of it was the goodness. It felt incredible to be exactly where she was, her body twinging in places it had never twinged before, her senses inundated with the presence of the man whom she was snuggled so closely against. This intimacy was as delicious as the lovemaking...well almost.

She had never realized how alone she'd been, even with her mom and her so close. This was different. This was a lover, someone who belonged to her, was with her and only her. Amazing.

She carefully shifted her hand against satin smooth skin, gently exploring the contours of his torso. While it felt completely perfect, it also awed her to be here, held by him even as his body slept...to have the freedom to touch.

As a model, others had the freedom to touch her. Not in any lewd way, but dressers, designers...even patrons at a trunk show would feel the texture of the fabrics she wore...her body the mannequin beneath the clothes. However, she rarely touched others. And was only now realizing that salient fact.

Beneath the friendly, confident facade she'd developed for her career, she was really rather reserved.

She hugged her mom...even hugged some of her friends in greeting, but not often and this was definitely different. This was having the right to explore the secrets of Miguel's body, and even more—to touch him with possessive affection. What she was doing right now didn't feel sexual… she was curious about how he felt, wanted to learn him, but she was not feeling over-whelming passion at the moment. Just happiness.

A kind of burbling joy welling from deep inside that gave a nod to the loneliness she'd never acknowledged at the very same time it smoothed that loneliness away as if it had never been. Suddenly it was all so clear…she didn't have to choose between a relationship and her career. She could have both, had been silly to think for so many years that she couldn't.

Miguel would understand the demands of her job just as she understood the demands of his. They would both compromise and make this incredible gift given to them work.

She almost laughed aloud at herself, but kept it back. Okay, maybe she was getting ahead of the game plan. She'd always heard that men were slower to make these kinds of life choices and she was determined to give Miguel all the time he needed. She'd thought she was the one who would have to be con-vinced of the viability of a relationship and now that she realized it was not so, she felt remarkably, wonderfully free.

Free to love. Free to bask in happiness. Free to touch. How amazing was that? As her fingers traced the plains of his chest, distinguishing between the parts that had hair and those that were smooth to the touch, the heartbeat under her ear began to beat faster.

A delighted giggle spilled forth from her mouth and she deliberately explored areas she'd already learned were sensitive, like the brown disks of his nipples.

The hand on her back started moving, caressing her with slow, lazy circles that elongated to ovals until on the downward dip, that big hand brushed over the curve of her bottom.

Her breath hitched, the feelings of security and contentment morphing into something else entirely, and yet also still there under the sexual desire wakening inside her.

"This is nice," he said in a voice husky from sleep.

She smiled against him. "Yes, it is. Wonderfully nice."

He made a beautifully masculine sound of enjoyment and his hand dipped between her legs, touching her intimately.

Her body gave an involuntary jerk and she gasped.

He stilled. "Was that a sound of pleasure, surprise or discomfort?"

She pressed a kiss against his chest. "All of the above, I think."

"Explain."

She knew which part he wanted elucidated. "It stings…just a little."

"Hmmm." He shifted and moved her onto her back then leaned down and kissed her. It wasn't a short kiss, but it wasn't long and involved, either. More like a nice-waking-up-next-to-you sort of salute. "The casino it is."

"But I want—"

He pressed his finger over her lips, cutting her off. "A small amount of self-denial now will make for a much more pleasure filled time together over the next two weeks."

His erection was pressing against her hip.

She moved against it. "I don't think the self-denial bit is so small."

He laughed.

"I really think I'll be all right."

"Trust me to know what is best."

"Why, have you made love to many

virgins?" she asked, suddenly hating the very idea, but not about to admit it.

"No. None in fact, but my father has every expectation I will marry one and gave both my brother and myself an equally disturbing talk on our sixteenth birthdays."

"You compared notes?"

"Yes. It is much easier to discuss such things with one another, believe me."

"I can imagine." As close as she and her mom were, Helen Taylor had opted to buy Amber a book on her emerging teen sexuality when she went into puberty. When Amber had had more questions, her mom had bought her more books.

She certainly appreciated the approach as it had avoided any awkward discussions like the kind Miguel was talking about.

"He really told you to show self-denial after the first time."

"If there was any tenderness, or residual soreness, yes."

"You mean there isn't always?"

"I do not know, but I imagine not all initiations into lovemaking are as energetic as your own."

"You mean wild?"

His eyes darkened. "That, too."

"I have no problem believing that. I don't think even longtime lovers can usually boast their intimacy is so explosive."

"You would know?"

"Other models talk."

He laughed. "Yes, well, we'll have to be more careful in future. Our after play rendered the condom not quite so protective."

"What do you mean?"

"It did not break, but there was some leakage at the top. I don't think anything to be worried about."

She nodded, agreeing. "It's not right for my cycle, either."

Miguel relaxed almost imperceptibly. "That is good to know."

Only then did she realize that despite his words to the contrary, he'd been worried. But he hadn't wanted to ruin her first time with concerns. That was just…really sweet. And then there was the way he was worried about hurting her by making love again too soon.

She beamed up at him. "You are a very nice man, Miguel Menendez."

"Thank you, *querida*. I try."

They both laughed.

* * *

Miguel enjoyed the casino for the simple fact that it drew a hugely varied clientele, many of whom were not native to the area and therefore affording him a certain amount of anonymity. An added bonus was the realization that Amber had no clue how to gamble. However, it was clear she enjoyed learning… immensely.

And he enjoyed teaching her. It fed his ego to have her turning to him frequently for advice. Upon discovering her novice status, he made the decision not to gamble himself. He wanted to focus completely on enhancing her amusement at his long enjoyed pastime. In doing so, he found himself having more fun than he ever had at one of his favorite haunts.

Though, for the first time in memory, he did not like the looks his beautiful companion received from other men. While he had never dated another woman for the trophy factor hanging off of his arm, he had never been bothered that they drew .attention, either. It had fed his Spanish pride even if it had not been a reason for being with them.

Tonight, all he felt was annoyance when other men looked, smiled and damn it to hell if one had not just asked her if she wanted some help.

Miguel put his arm around her waist possessively. "She has my expert advice to lean on," he said with a smile that nowhere near reached his eyes and in a voice that he used on business enemies rather than associates.

The tall, well dressed blond man, an American by his accent, blinked. He slid his gaze to Amber. "That right? You don't want any more help learning this here little game?"

She shook her head, her smile too sweet for Miguel's comfort. "No, thank you. You know what they say about too many cooks in the kitchen spoiling the broth. Too much advice does the same thing in things like this."

"Well, you sure you want to keep the one you got, sugar?"

Miguel stiffened at the man's use of an endearment with his Amber. Forget that he often called women by endearments that meant nothing to him. This was his woman. For the next two weeks anyway.

Amber just laughed. "My best friend in college was from Texas. She said the men were friendly—she was right."

"Some might consider certain types of

friendliness as unacceptably forward," Miguel inserted with lethal coolness.

The Texan smiled, showing a mouth full of even, white teeth. "Point taken, mister. I'll just mosey on to warmer climes."

He nodded to Amber and Miguel got the distinct impression he would have been more comfortable tipping a cowboy hat.

Amber slid Miguel a sidelong glance. "Feeling possessive?"

"After this afternoon, do you blame me?"

"Not at all. When other women look at you, I want to get physical and I'm definitely not the type."

"I am glad to hear I am not alone in this strange reaction."

"Me, too."

He smiled, this time the expression far more genuine than when he'd used it on the blond man.

She turned back to her cards and proceeded to lose the next hand. Once new cards had been dealt, she peeked at hers and then, biting her lip in that adorable way she did, she turned questioning blue-green eyes to him. "What do you think I should do?"

She was playing black jack and had been

dealt two face cards. She could split her hand, hoping to hit twenty-one with one or both face cards, or hold with the hope that no one else at the table would get the winning combination. "That depends on what kind of risk you prefer to take."

"I'm not big into risk taking at all…or at least I wasn't before I met you."

He grinned. "Good to hear it."

"Is it?"

"Yes. A man likes to know he has a singular effect on his woman."

She grinned. "You do that. A very singular effect. As I'm sure you know."

Then she went suddenly shy, dropping her gaze. He could not stop himself from leaning down to press a brief kiss to her lips even though they were in a crowded public venue and he had seen a photographer earlier. It just didn't seem to matter. Besides, he wasn't worried about their privacy being invaded too much. Pictures were one thing…names were another and he'd done what he could to protect hers from getting out.

She ended up staying with the cards she'd been dealt and winning the pot. "Oh, this is fun, Miguel."

"Yes, it is." Watching her was truly pleasurable.

"I can't believe I've never gambled before."

"Well, it's not quite as fun when you're losing consistently."

"Oh, no, I suppose not. I suppose that's the primary reason I've never gambled. I'm not a big fan of trying things it's so easy to lose at."

"You are adept at stacking the deck in your favor."

"Don't talk like that here. They'll think I'm a card shark."

"No one is going to believe such a lovely woman could be anything but honest."

She snorted inelegantly and he laughed out loud. "Throughout history beauty has been used to hide deception. I don't think anyone looks at my photogenic face and automatically thinks, *there goes an honest woman*."

"Ah, but not only are you a stunningly lovely woman, but you glow with innocence."

"Not anymore," she quipped.

And he almost choked on his own breath. The little minx. "Still very innocent, I think."

"I suppose you'll have to fix that, won't you?" She flirted up at him through her eyelashes.

"It will be my pleasure."

"And mine."

"Count on it."

"Wow...this is just so strange, Miguel."

"What?"

Vulnerability and something like awe shimmered in her sea-green depths. "Being together...being with you."

"Funny." He squeezed her waist. "It does not feel odd to me at all."

"Truly?" She was looking at him, all serious and questioning.

He clamped his jaw on his initial flip reply and thought about it. "Well, perhaps a bit."

She smiled as if he'd given her a gift and he was very glad he'd taken the moment for honesty. He only wished they had more than two weeks for the sense of strangeness to wear off. They were both going to feel like something was left undone when he had to leave for Prague.

But it could not be helped.

As they had agreed earlier, sometimes you simply had to seize the moment.

He was thinking about the time limitation to their affair late that night as he lay in bed beside her sleeping form. They had retrieved her things from her hotel on the way home from the casino and he'd convinced her to go to sleep without making love again. Gratifyingly she had balked, but he had been adamant. He wanted to give her body time to heal.

If that left him hard and aching while he watched her sleep, so be it. She was too precious to allow his libido to override what he knew to be good for her.

Normally when he could not sleep, he would have gotten up to work, but he did not want to leave her. By the saints, he had it bad. Was that because she'd been a virgin? He'd never really believed it made a difference, but he felt more possessively toward her than he had any previous lover.

It must be because of her innocence.

The thought of breaking off their relationship when he went to Prague filled him with more than frustration at an affair that would end to early. Unreasoning anger beat a steady tattoo in his chest. He did not want to leave the field open for some other man to come in and claim the passion he had awakened in *his* Amber.

But there was no other tenable option.

It would not be fair to her or himself to be

tied to a long distance relationship. Attempting such a thing with the commitments they each had to their work would be impossible. They would only be able to see each other when she could get time off between jobs and considering the fact this was her first vacation in more than a year, he had little hope such circumstances would arise often enough to suit either of them.

The business commitments he had agreed to shoulder for his family's company in Prague would preclude him leaving Russia for six months, maybe even a year. He might be able to arrange a flying visit or two to California, but nothing more. Not enough to maintain a committed, exclusive relationship.

He could not be sure of his ability to go without sex if they had a long separation. He never had before. He loved sexual intimacy and needed the stress release it provided when business got extra intense. Now that Amber knew what she'd been missing, he did not think she would sublimate her sensuality with work so effectively, either.

No. A long distance relationship was only asking for trouble and heartache for both of them.

He could not back out of his commitment to his family. Such an option was unthinkable. Well, he had thought of it and then discarded it. He had never let the company down before and family pride and duty demanded he not start now.

He could not ask Amber to come to Prague with him. Not even for a couple of months, though the temptation was acute.

It would be absolutely unfair to her. Her career was just heating up and she would be very busy, especially once a few well placed recommendations were made by Miguel's ad campaign manager. He'd spoken to the man earlier that day and made it clear that Menendez Enterprises would be grateful to others (including his own employee) who saw the same potential in Amber Taylor that they had. She wouldn't want him to do that, which was why he hadn't told her.

But having friends in business never hurt.

He sighed and touched the top slope of her breast exposed by the dipping neckline on her silk sleepshirt. Leaving this woman would be hard, but he had no choice. A clean break at the end of their time together was the only way, but that didn't mean he couldn't maximize the time they did have together.

Unwilling to dwell any longer on unpalatable facts that could not be changed, he forced himself to climb from the bed leaving her seductive warmth behind. Work would afford distraction from his chaotic thoughts. Sometimes toiling in the wee hours was the best way to accomplish a lot in a short period. If he was going to maximize the precious little time he did have with Amber, he needed to get rid of as many work obligations as possible.

CHAPTER EIGHT

AN HOUR and a half later, Miguel sat up from where he'd been working at the coffee table in the living room and stretched. He had delegated all the responsibilities he could without letting anyone down, answered e-mails he would have had to at the office later, and even had two IM sessions with international associates that took care of any communication he would have had to have with them the following week.

He was closing his computer when a slight sound to his left caught his attention. He looked up.

Amber stood a few short feet from the sofa, her golden hair a messy halo around her sleep softened features, her slight curves accented by the silky nightshirt. She smiled softly. "Hi."

He snapped the laptop shut and leaned back on the sofa, his long legs stretched out before him. If he got within touching distance, he was going to touch…and a whole lot more. "Hi, yourself. What are you doing up, *querida*?"

She shrugged. "I woke and you were gone. I decided to find you." She looked down at the closed laptop. "Working?"

"Yes."

"Couldn't sleep or stuff that couldn't wait?"

"A little of both, but mostly sleeping within touching distance of temptation became too much."

She smiled and came to sit beside him, her feminine scent reaching out to wrap around him as she curled up facing him, one hand on his chest. "How's this for temptation?"

He groaned. "The sadistic streak is not something I expected."

"I'm not trying to hurt you."

"But you are tempting me…knowing I cannot follow through. Some might call that cruel." He called it too damn delicious.

"You know, I may have been a virgin less than twenty-four hours ago, but I am not ignorant." She rubbed her face against his chest, making a little humming sound.

"There are things we can do that do not require penetration."

"You have done these things?" he demanded, wondering why the prospect she had would bother him. It should not.

Then again, he did not think she would enjoy hearing about his past conquests.

"No, but I read about them."

"You *read* about them?"

"My mother's answer to sex education. Books."

"And what did you read about in these books?" The very idea of her telling him had him swelling with anticipation. He'd been semierect since bringing her back to the penthouse, so it took very little to tent the silk boxers he wore.

Her hand slid up his chest until one fingertip was over his hardening nipple. "I'd rather show you than tell you."

"I would very much like to hear you tell me. Are you too shy?"

She looked up at him. "Maybe."

"Would it help if I started?"

"You can't tell me what I read about."

He grinned at her affront. "But I can tell you what I know."

"Yes." The word gusted out on a soft sigh. "And you can tell me why you didn't suggest the other ways of touching yourself."

"I was afraid that I would not stop at the boundary that must be maintained for your body's recovery."

"Ohhhh…I like being that much a temptation to you."

"I also like the fact you are such a temptation."

She laughed, the sound musical and sweet. And extremely sexy. "So, are you going to start?"

"Shall we make it a game? I say something, then you?"

"Hmmm…I think we can make it a little more interesting than that."

"More interesting?"

His little ex-virgin was definitely full of surprises.

"Right." She considered him for several seconds, her lower lip caught between her teeth. "Okay, what about if you tell me something I can do to give you pleasure and I do it?"

"And then you will tell me something that will give you pleasure and I am supposed to do it?" He liked the sound of this game. A lot.

"Yes." Though crimson dusted her lovely cheekbones. The sweet innocent was definitely more comfortable with the first part of the game.

"A man has many areas of his body that give pleasure, though we tend to concentrate on one particular organ."

"Hmmm, yes…maybe we should add another rule…you have to give me at least three other options before directing me to touch you…um…" She licked her lips and dipped her gaze to his lap. *"Down there."*

He manfully held back his laughter at her awkwardness. He found it endearing, but did not think she would read his amusement in that light. "I agree, but *you* cannot go more than three turns without directing me to touch you somewhere between your legs."

She closed her eyes as if praying, but nodded. "All right. Deal."

Then they looked at each other in silence while anticipation built between them.

He took her hand and put it on his inner thigh, brushing the back of her fingers. "Touch me there and you will make me weep with pleasure."

"How?"

"Any way you like."

She started by caressing him lightly through the silk of his boxers, tracing the contours of his muscles and sending shivers through him. It took all his control not to close his legs and trap her hand when it strayed near his sex. He made a strangled sound and forced his thighs to remain apart.

She looked up into his eyes, her own pupils dilated with passion. "You're not weeping."

He husked out a laugh. "That was merely an expression of speech, but believe me, you are achieving the desired reaction."

She bit her lip and narrowed her eyes, going completely still as if thinking. Then she increased the pressure of her touch, kneading his thigh through the silk, the sensation more stimulating than he would have expected. Every touch felt like it zinged straight to his groin, pulsing through his erect shaft with teasing pleasure.

When she stopped, he had to take a deep breath and let it out before he could speak. "Now it is your turn to tell me."

"I'm not done."

"What?"

"I'm still learning this thigh touching technique."

"You have it down," he insisted. Any more and he was going to lose his mind. Or weep for real.

But she shook her head and slipped her hand inside the leg of his shorts to touch bare skin.

He hissed his enjoyment while she moaned a little. The touch through silk had been erotic, but this was like being branded with her personal fire. And she acted like she could continue to touch that small area on his body for what remained of the night.

"We are going to have to institute a new rule," he said from between gritted teeth.

"What? A rule?" She looked up at him dazed.

"Yes. A rule. A time limit." He gently removed her hand, making a sound suspiciously close to a whimper as he did so and then grabbed his watch from the table and set the timer. "Three minute maximum per touch."

"So, you think it's been three minutes?" she asked with a heated look.

"More. Definitely longer."

"It's my turn then, hmm?"

"Yes."

"All right." She took a breath, as if girding herself to say what she wanted. "I read that every area of the body can be an erogenous zone if touched the right way."

"Okay then…touch my face."

Her *face?*

She must have read the shock in his expression because she smiled shyly. "I love the way it feels when you brush my hair back from my temple, or caress my cheek. I want to see if more touching will roll into the realm of the sensual or if there is an area of my body that isn't conducive to making love."

"I will show you that it is. Close your eyes."

She did, her body vibrating with clear anticipation for the first touch. He made it an ultralight kiss against her brow…then moved his mouth in soft nibbles down to her cheekbone and along her jaw. She was shivering in seconds and by the time he was feathering kisses over her eyelids, he was sure she would concede the point.

"It works," she said breathlessly. "And you didn't even kiss my mouth."

"That would have been too easy."

"You are such a competitor," she said on a groan. Her eyes opened slowly, as if she was forcing them to obey her inner command and her breath was coming in shallow gasps. "What next?"

He knew exactly what he wanted. "Your mouth on my stomach." He settled back, going completely still and silent, waiting for her to touch him.

She turned to fiddle with his watch, resetting the timer and then faced him again, reaching out to touch his stomach with barely there caresses.

He had to bite back a reminder that she was not using her mouth. He wanted to know what she would do.

She leaned forward to hover over him, her hands never stopping the gentle touching. "Your body is so amazing to me, you're strong everywhere. Before I came to find you, I lay in bed thinking about you, about how you touch me, fantasizing about you kissing me all over."

The scent of her arousal testified to the veracity of her words and he had to clench his jaw tight to hold back a moan. She was such a mixture of innocence and frank sensuality. She enthralled him.

Then she kissed him, right below his belly

button, opening her mouth to suck, bringing blood to the surface and no doubt leaving a mark of her possession.

A rumble of passion shook his chest and his mouth opened of its own volition on a hoarse grunt.

She rained kisses all over his stomach, flicking her tongue out to taste his skin every few seconds. He was moaning when his watch started beeping.

Amber sat up, her eyes shining with both desire and satisfaction. "Time's up."

He nodded, taking a deep breath before husking out, "Now you." She impacted him like no other.

Her eyes gleamed with mischief. "Use your mouth someplace unexpected." She climbed onto his lap, straddling his thighs, her naked, damp curls settling over his pulsingly hard flesh. "I'll even make it easier for you."

"This is supposed to be easy on me?" he choked out.

"Easy access."

"What if I wanted to lick your feet?"

"That wouldn't be a big surprise. I mean kissing someone's feet is what you'd expect when trying for the unexpected, so it isn't anymore. Know what I mean?"

He laughed, shocked at how much fun he was having. He was used to sex being physically intense, cathartic even, but not *fun*. "Set the timer," he growled.

She reached behind her and did it, tossing the watch onto the couch cushions beside them.

Then, he prepared to do the unexpected. He grabbed her face and kissed her lips, delving inside when her mouth parted on a surprised gasp. He kissed her until the timer went off on his watch and a little beyond.

When he stopped, she lifted her head, dazed looking. "I wasn't expecting that. I thought you'd kiss me someplace funny like my elbow or something."

"I know."

"You're devious."

"Yes."

"I think I like that."

He grinned and then groaned as she shifted just enough to make his already aching erection swell further. He grabbed her hips and tilted upward, letting her feel the effect she had on him. "I want you to rock against me."

She gasped and sighed and closed her eyes

for a second. "That would be touching you there. Not for another turn," she said between breathy little gasps.

"Fine, then I want you to touch my chest like you were doing when I woke earlier…before the casino," he clarified, in case she didn't remember in her aroused state.

"I can do that." She straightened, forcing their intimate flesh to more contact. "I think."

"Try."

She did, caressing him and kissing him and not even remembering to reset the watch. They were both panting when she finally lifted her head.

He looked at her and tried to grasp the last thread of his thought process. "So, what do you want me to do?"

"Make love to me."

"Not on the menu." But he wanted to. Badly.

She pouted and he had to kiss her again. Then he was pushing her back on the couch and disposing of her nightshirt so he could do what she'd said she fantasized about….kiss her all over.

Amber screamed as she climaxed from the incredible sensation of having her most intimate flesh invaded by Miguel's tongue. He'd done this before, but this time he'd used his mouth to sensitize every centimeter of her body first. And she was a quivering mess. At least inside. Outside, she was sweaty, her hot skin radiating with spent pleasure.

Miguel lifted her into his arms. "Time for bed now."

"What about you?"

"I found my pleasure in giving you yours. Literally." He laid her on the bed. "I'll be back in a minute. I have to clean up."

"Oh, wow…"

She was barely coherent when he returned to the bed to pull her into his arms and glad he didn't expect her to bathe again, though she'd need a nice long shower in the morning.

"Was wonderful," she slurred.

"Tomorrow, when I can be inside you will be even better."

"Might not survive it."

His rich chuckle was the last sound she heard as she slipped into sleep.

The next morning, Amber woke alone. She wasn't surprised because Miguel had woken her before leaving to tell her to get more rest and that he would be back later in the morning. She'd promptly gone back to sleep and just woken.

The clock on the bedside table said it was just going on nine, which was hours later than she'd slept in for months. But considering how late they'd gotten back from the casino and what they'd done in the middle of the night, well…maybe she could be forgiven for sleeping in a little.

She took her time showering and drying her hair, stopping at one point facing the mirror, wrapped in a towel. She let the towel drop to take her usual inventory, determine if she needed to work on any particular part of her body before the next job and ended up staring rather dazedly instead.

Small marks on her breasts, stomach and thigh attested to Miguel's oral attentions. Her nipples beaded immediately as memory of those attentions washed over her. Her breasts were no rounder than they had been the day before and yet somehow they seemed more prominent to her. When she looked at her waist and hips, she did not see artistic proportion, but curves meant to entice her lover.

It had been a long time since she had

looked in the mirror and seen anything but a tool for her trade. So long in fact, that she could not remember the last time. Now she was seeing a woman capable of giving and receiving immense sensual pleasure. A woman capable of love.

Miguel returned a little before noon. He made good on his promise to squire Amber around Barcelona, taking her to *Parc Güell* to see the incredible whimsy designed by Antoni Gaudi. The Snake Bench was incredible. Pictures she'd seen of the yards long, winding mosaic bench could not do it justice.

"This is incredible," she said with a sigh, enjoying the panoramic view from her perch on one of the interior curves of the bench.

"Yes. Gaudi was a man with vision."

"Not everyone thinks so."

"Not everyone gets the Modernistic Style."

She smiled. "But we do."

"Yes, we share this in common."

They actually liked a lot of the same things and shared many of the same interests. Miguel had been able to answer numerous questions she'd had on Barcelona, its people and its history and had proven himself not only capable, but enthusiastic in doing so.

"I don't remember having so much fun with another person when traveling," she said with a grin. Not the smile she used for the camera, but a happy expression that started deep in her chest. "Not even my mom."

"Your mother, for all her paragon list of virtues you've shared with me, is still a mother. I am, however, your lover and a native of this city that fascinates you so."

He proved the lover part again later that afternoon, turning siesta time once again into an exercise in discovering her latent sensuality. They spent several days seeing Barcelona and its surrounding area. On one occasion, they went to a nearby beach and he surprised her by arranging a hotel room right on the water.

She loved it.

They walked hand in hand on the pebbly beach near dusk. She missed watching the sun set over the water, but Miguel had promised to wake her to enjoy the sun rising over the sea the next morning. "I promise you, the colors are spectacular."

"I'm sure they are."

They were watching the sunrise the next morning when Miguel said, "You truly love the water, yes?"

"Oh, yes. I don't think I could ever live anywhere that wasn't close to the ocean."

"Perhaps you are part mermaid."

She laughed. "Maybe."

"I have arranged a surprise for you, I hope you will like it."

"I'm sure I will." Just the thought of him going to the trouble to surprise her made her feel cherished.

They were standing at the rail on his yacht when it started moving before the final shoe dropped on her surprise.

"We're moving."

"Yes."

"For a day cruise?" she asked, anticipation shimmering through her.

"You said you did not need to return to California for another nine days."

"We aren't cruising for that whole time, are we?" she asked in an awed voice.

For Miguel to take that kind of time off to spend alone with her was just…it was… totally phenomenal. She would never have expected it.

"I will still have to take care of certain business matters, but I have cleared my schedule sufficiently to make the long cruise possible."

"Wow. It's like a honeymoon." Then she bit her lip and blushed at what she'd said. No matter how wonderful the last few days had been, she and Miguel still weren't anywhere near a place they could talk about that kind of long-term future together. "Scratch that, I'd draw and quarter any husband of mine who worked intermittently on the honeymoon," she said, laughing off her words with a joke.

"Neither of us is in a place to think about that sort of thing," he replied, his lips quirking.

"By that sort of thing, you mean marriage… or honeymoons?"

"Do they not usually go together?"

"I would say so, yes."

"This…" He swept his hand out in an arc, encompassing the yacht and the now moving water beneath them. "Is an opportunity to make the most of our time together. No unintentional overtones, nothing but you and I enjoying one another and something beautifully unique."

"You're right. I know you have to work,

but can we leave our jobs and the rest of our lives on the shore?" It sounded so good, to spend an entire week not thinking about her career or focusing on business in any way. It would be a true vacation, of both the mind and the body.

"I solemnly vow to dismiss my responsibilities from my mind except those short hours each day I have to dedicate to them."

"That works for me." Out of sight…out of mind, or something like that.

CHAPTER NINE

AND it did work. They cruised the open sea mostly, staying close enough to shore for some spectacular views, but also offering tons of privacy. There was a small crew on board that took care of everything, just as if they were staying in a luxury all inclusive hotel. But better.

The yacht…the crew…the privacy…all added up to something very special. And he'd made it happen because their relationship was unique.

Amber spent a lot of time smiling over the next week.

They were cruising back toward port when Miguel came up to her standing at the rail. The warm sun beat against her skin while a gentle breeze kept her hair flying around her face.

A strong arm wrapped around her waist. "We are close to home."

"How long until we reach port?"

"A couple of hours, maybe less."

"Our idyll is over then?"

"Yes, or close to it." He kissed the top of her head. "We need to talk."

She turned into his arms. "Not yet. I don't want to discuss the future yet. We've still got two hours before our special time is up."

The two hours stretched to the evening, when they decided to have dinner aboard the yacht and then afterward making love came all too naturally and they spent the night on the moored yacht as well.

The next morning was rushed—Miguel had business that had been waiting for his return to port and Amber had to finish packing for her early afternoon flight. The plan was for Miguel to see her off at the airport, but he was called into a high level meeting and was unable to get away.

Her cell phone chirped while she was waiting to board her flight. Half the plane had boarded already.

"Hello?" she said into the phone, juggling her carry-on and purse.

"Amber, it is Miguel."

"I didn't think you'd get to call before I had to leave."

"I snuck out of the meeting room with the excuse of needing a bio break."

She laughed. "Thank you."

"I miss you already."

"Me, too."

"We have not talked about the future yet. There is something I need to tell you."

They announced her row number for boarding. She turned away from the shuffling line of air passengers. "Yes?"

"I leave for Prague in a week's time."

"Wow." She'd always wanted to go to Russia. "How long will you be gone?"

"It is for a long-term project."

"I see." She supposed that wasn't so very different than him living in Spain. The flights to visit would be longer was all. The last call for boarding was announced. "I've got to go, Miguel."

He said something that sounded like a curse. "I was thinking about flying out to California next week."

Suddenly she felt as light as air. "I'd like that."

"I will see you then."

"Great." She hung up, grinning, and sprinted for the boarding gate.

Her mom was at the airport to pick Amber up. They talked about Miguel the whole way home.

"Honey, I'm so glad to see you so happy."

"He's wonderful, Mom. I don't know how we're going to work out our relationship long distance—especially since he'll be in Prague for a while, but it's worth the effort. I didn't think you really could fall in love so fast, but I did."

"Did you tell him?"

"No. I guess I'm a little afraid it's not real and he hasn't said anything."

Her mom nodded and gave her a conspiratorial wink. "Men often find it difficult to express their feelings verbally."

"Did Dad?"

Helen's expression softened with memories. "No. He moved too fast for me, in fact. He proposed on our second date, I didn't agree for almost two months after. I was cautious." Her face showed old grief. "If I'd known how little time we would have together, I would have dragged him before a minister on our first date."

"I thought about that…when I decided to risk, well…getting intimate with Miguel. It wasn't a conscious thing, but I had this feeling that I had to seize the moment. We even made a joke about it, Miguel and I. My feeling must have come from a subconscious thinking how you lost Dad so early."

"I'm glad you took a risk, sweetheart."

"Me, too," Amber said with a smile.

She was even gladder when Miguel called later to make sure she'd arrived all right. It was the middle of the night for him—or rather early morning, but he made no effort to keep the conversation short. They talked about what he would be doing in Prague and the trunk show she'd returned to California for.

They hung up when her mom came in to remind her that she had to be at the fitting for the trunk show very early the next morning. "You don't want dark circles under your eyes when you meet with the designer, sweetie. He might take it into his head to put one of the other models in your place."

"You need your rest, *querida*," Miguel said, clearly having heard her mother. "I will call to let you know when I will be in California."

"All right," she grumbled, annoyed for the first time in memory with the intrusion of having to do what was best for her career.

She was exercising to clear her mind and stretch her limbs after the grueling fitting the next day when the doorbell rang. Her mom hadn't said she'd been expecting anyone, but it could be a neighbor, or even one of her mom's clients. Voices from the living room drew Amber's attention and she decided to investigate.

She stopped still in the doorway, trying to assimilate the scene before her. Her mom was sitting on the sofa with an attractive man about her age. He had his arm around her shoulders and she was crying.

Amber had never seen Helen Taylor cry, much less allow a man to touch her. She was riveted to her spot by the tableau as her mother spoke in voice made choppy with tears. "I knew this day would come, but I kept hoping it wouldn't. That wasn't fair of me. I know. I've been so selfish."

The man gave her mom a look filled with his own grief mixed with compassion. "Tell me why you took my daughter."

Everything inside Amber froze. What was

the man talking about and why wasn't her mom telling him he was crazy?

Her mom choked out, "I…" but got no further.

Helen was ready to fly apart; Amber could see it in the way she held herself. She couldn't let that happen. Her mom hated losing her cool, but especially in front of strangers. "Mom, what's going on?"

Movement to her left caught Amber's gaze. Another woman similar to her own age was there. Amber's heart slammed in her chest as she took in an almost perfect mirror image to herself. A tall, dark haired man stood behind the lookalike, his posture obviously protective.

Eyes identical in color and shape to her own glistened with tears. "Amber…"

"Who are you?" Amber asked, deeply bothered that the stranger seemed to know who she was while she was so completely at a loss, but she strived not to let it show.

"I'm…" But like Amber's mom, this woman didn't seem to know what to say and stopped after only one word, too.

"She's your sister." Her mom had said that. *Her* mom, who had no other children besides Amber.

"My sister?" Amber shook her head, pain that she didn't understand a band squeezing around her heart. "No. That's not possible. You didn't give birth to twins. I checked. I always felt like something was missing, you know?" She was babbling, but darn it… nothing made sense. "So, I checked and there wasn't another birth record. I was the only baby born to Helen and Leonard Taylor."

The younger man said, "Miss Taylor, perhaps you should sit down."

"Who are you?" Amber demanded, stepping away from him, concentrating on keeping her game face on.

"I am your sister's fiancé, Sandor Christofides."

"The shipping tycoon?"

"You read the financial pages?"

"Sometimes. When I'm bored on a shoot." Why was he asking something so mundane when her entire world was shattering around her? "And you're George Wentworth," she said to the man seated beside her mother.

Who were these people? Okay, so she knew who they were, but *who* were they *in relation to her?* What were they doing here in her home, talking to her mother?

The older man stood. "I'm…" He cleared his throat. "Yes, I'm George Wentworth."

Her mom sat up, wiped at her tears and then dried her hands on her jeans and put her arms out, like she had so many times when Amber needed comfort. Only, she didn't need comforting right now…did she? "Come here, baby. I have to tell you something."

Unwilling to refuse her mom who was in obvious emotional distress, Amber walked slowly toward her. Mr. Wentworth stepped back, moving to sit in a chair close to the sofa. Amber let her mother pull her down to sit on the couch.

The woman her mom had said was Amber's sister held her head at the same angle as George Wentworth. Were they related?

Amber met the woman's gaze. "You look just like me."

"Almost." A small deprecatory smile and shrug accompanied the word.

Amber considered that. She, better than another, was prepared to catalog a list of superficial differences. "Your hair is darker. You don't highlight it at all."

"No."

"It's shorter, too." A little anyway.

"Yes. And my eyebrows have their natural shape and I weigh at least ten pounds more than you. I don't dress as trendily and I'm not fond of running," she said, naming Amber's favorite form of exercise. "But I love old movies, we wear the same size shoe and I prefer silver over gold jewelry as well."

Amber's mom made a sound of distress that echoed the chaotic feelings exploding inside her. But Amber had years experience projecting for the camera and she did not let any of her inner turmoil show on her face. She was strong enough to get through whatever this was and she had a feeling that her newfound happiness, her safe world was about to be blown apart...

She took her mom's hand. "What's the matter, Mom?"

"Please don't hate me, Amber. I deserve it, I know I do, but I can handle anything except that."

Shock kept her mouth from uttering her initial denial. What was her mom saying? What was she admitting to?

"No one is going to hate you, Mrs. Taylor. We're going to work through this," George Wentworth said in a firm but kind tone.

"I could never hate you," Amber vowed.

"Before you came into the room, Mr. Wentworth asked a question. He wanted…" Her mom stopped, collected herself and went on. "He wanted to know why I'd stolen his daughter."

Amber's body jolted as if it had taken a mortal blow. "What?"

Then her mom started talking, telling a story that made a terrible kind of sense. She'd lost her baby due to the same accident that had killed her beloved husband. She'd gone into some kind of postpartum depression or temporary psychosis. She'd been there at the hospital the night the woman who gave birth to Amber and her sister had died.

Something had snapped inside her and Helen Taylor had kidnapped one of the babies, believing she was her own Amber, instead of the child of the deceased woman. Mr. Wentworth nodded, as if he understood how this terrible thing could have happened. Amber thought he had to be one of the most amazing men she'd ever met. He wasn't screaming or threatening, or anything. Wow.

"Don't ask me how I managed to get you out of the hospital because I don't remember.

When I got you home, all the baby stuff was still there, I thought you were my little Amber." Her mom's voice cracked. "I loved you so much and you were all I had left."

Amber put her arm around her mom's shoulder, giving back some of the comfort her mom had extended to her over the years. "It's okay, Mom."

Her mom shook her head and kept talking. She'd lived and believed the fantasy for five years.

"But something made you remember," Amber said gently.

"I saw an article on George Wentworth in a business weekly." Her mom looked around at the rest of the people in the room. "I'm a financial analyst."

"We know," George said quietly.

"Of course." She took another deep breath and clenched her trembling hands together. "The article mentioned the disappearance of your daughter and suddenly *I knew*. I couldn't remember taking her, but I remembered my baby dying and knew that the little girl who I loved more than my own life belonged to someone else."

"I don't understand...you would have

taken me back. Mom, I know you…" No way would her mom have kept a child from her father once she realized the truth.

"Yes. I tried." Her mom looked at her with an expression in her hazel eyes that broke Amber's heart. "I had to investigate him. I couldn't just hand you over to some stranger, even if he was your biological father."

The words that followed did not match the man being so kind and compassionate right now. Her mom painted a picture of George Wentworth as an unforgiving, merciless business shark and terrible father—cold, emotionally distant and uninterested in his remaining daughter.

Helen looked at Mr. Wentworth…Amber's dad…as if she couldn't quite believe he was the man she was describing and then back to Amber. "You were such a loving little girl and affectionate. You would have shriveled up and died under that kind of care. I couldn't do it. I couldn't give you back. And he never changed. I kept tabs and watched his daughter Eleanor be sent to boarding school when she was barely eight years old."

Helen's eyes filled with tears as she met Eleanor's gaze. "It hurt so much to see you treated like that. I loved your sister with all my heart and you by proxy. I couldn't change your life, but I couldn't let your father do the same thing to Amber."

"I understand," Amber's twin said as if she really meant it. "I'm glad my sister escaped having a childhood like mine. I'm glad you were there to love her."

Amber couldn't accept that and didn't see how Eleanor could. "But she needed me. If you'd given me back, we would have had each other."

"I thought of that and I just couldn't sacrifice your happiness for hers." Her mom buried her face in her hands and started to sob. "I'm sorry."

The man she now knew was her dad moved to sit on the other side of the woman who she had always believed was her mom. He pulled her into his arms and just held her. Amber couldn't help loving him right then. No matter what kind of father he'd been to Eleanor, he was being exactly what both she and her mom needed right now.

"If my biological father was such a horrible man why isn't he threatening prison and yelling at her?" Amber asked

Eleanor, trying to reconcile the past with the present.

"He almost died a couple of weeks ago and it changed him. I think he really loves me finally and I know he's going to love you."

The words shredded something in Amber's heart. Her sister was still unsure of her dad's love. That had to hurt so much. "But, Mom?" she couldn't help asking.

"Nothing is going to happen to your mom. Dad doesn't want to hurt her and neither do I. I only want to know you. I'd like to know her, too, if she'll let me. She was a good mom to you. She took care of you and after hearing her story, I'm convinced she didn't do anything with malice."

"Are you for real?" Amber asked, impressed to death by the loving compassion in this woman everyone claimed was her sister. "Nobody reacts like that to something like this."

Sandor laughed, hugging his fiancée. "Ellie is a special woman."

Ellie? She liked that better than Eleanor…it was warmer. And she was happy someone seemed to have that special of a relationship with her sister. Amber had taken her mom's love as a given her whole life. She couldn't imagine growing up the way Ellie had.

"I'm glad." Her control cracked for a second and her chin wobbled, but she got it under control. "I don't want my mom hurt," she reiterated.

"She won't be," her dad said with conviction she thought she could trust. "She did better by my daughter than I did. I stopped looking for you after only a year. I have no excuse for that. I was a rotten father to your sister, but she loved me in spite of it."

"There are worse fathers than you were, much worse," Ellie said and Amber wanted to hug her.

She couldn't, though...they hadn't been raised as sisters. They had nothing but genes and a past they had to come to terms with between them. She was really glad Sandor was there to hold her sister the way she couldn't.

"Thank you, sweetheart," George said, "but when I remember the times your eyes so like your mother's begged me to show a spark of affection and then I didn't...I'll never forgive myself."

"You hugged me sometimes."

Oh, man, those words just broke Amber's

heart all over again. The thing that hurt the most right in that moment was that she had spent a lifetime apart from this woman. Her sister. Not her mom's lies…they were understandable. Not being apart from her dad… she wasn't missing anything there, according to everyone else. But not being there for Ellie, that hurt.

Her dad looked like the words broke his heart, too. "I bet you remember every single time because those times were so rare."

"You really were a bastard," Amber breathed.

He flinched. "Yes. I was and I thank God Ellie never gave up on me. I've seen the error of my ways. I want to make up for them. I think we can build a family now. All of us, if you're willing."

"I won't leave my mom out."

"Like Ellie, I would appreciate the chance to get to know her, too."

At that her mom pulled out of his arms, wiping her face. She looked ravaged, but at peace and just a little bemused. "I've been so terrified for years. I can't believe things are happening this way."

"They wouldn't have…a few weeks ago."

"It's a good thing you didn't find me then," Amber quipped, but meaning it. Totally and completely.

The visit continued on a more positive note from there. Ellie didn't say much, but Amber didn't blame her. It was all so weird and really kind of scary. Her whole world was being turned topsy-turvy and it was taking all she had to keep it together and not show the pain splintering her insides to the people around her. Her mom didn't need it for sure, but she didn't want to share it with any of them really.

For lots of reasons. Her mind brought up an image of Miguel and she wished he was there. She envied Ellie Sandor's blatant support. He cared a lot for her sister and that was neat to see, something that helped Amber keep it together while she got to know her dad.

At some point, Sandor ordered dinner delivered. They all ate, still talking. It was late when he stood and said, "Ellie needs rest. It has been a very traumatic few weeks for her. Perhaps this visit can continue tomorrow?"

Amber looked at Ellie and bit her lip. "You haven't been talking much."

"I'm soaking it all in. I'm um…not used to being part of a family," she said.

Wow. Just…wow. Amber was the one who had been kidnapped, but Ellie was the one who had missed out on having a family. She promised to return the next day to visit some more and Amber was glad.

Their dad cleared his throat. "I would like to stay here a while longer…to talk out what I learned from my legal counsel with Helen in regard to the kidnapping and the statute of limitations and such."

"Is everything going to be okay?" Ellie asked. "She won't go to jail?"

"She will not. I have already put efforts into motion to assure that Helen suffers no more from the tragedy of her past."

Relief coursed through Amber. She wasn't sure what was going through her head about all of this, but one thing she knew…she did not want her mom hurt any more than she already was. "You did that before you even met us?" Amber asked.

"Yes."

"Thank you." She jumped up and hugged him and it was the strangest thing, but it was okay.

And he hugged her back and it felt good, if odd and a little scary. The idea of having more family…of her mom not really being her family. Only she was. Blood wasn't the only thing that made family ties. Her mom loved her and she had to cling to that knowledge when things got shaky. Right?

Her mom suggested she go to bed to be well rested for her trunk show the next day and Amber agreed. It was best to let her mom and her newfound father work out some things between them. And she needed some time to herself. Some time to think. To take it all in.

As promised, Ellie came back to visit the next day. But this time, she talked almost nonstop and Amber just loved her to death. She was a really special person, working in public employment counseling and trying to help people even though she didn't have to work at all.

And something that was really strange, but Ellie saw herself as average in looks. Amber had made a career on her beauty, which was identical to her sister's, so she had laughed out loud at her sister's comment to that effect.

Ellie had been bemused, Sandor amused and their dad had simply said, "I told you so."

It was funny, and kind of wonderful. She hoped Miguel would be able to make it to

California before her family flew back to the East Coast. She wanted to share this whole thing with him so much, needed him to feel more grounded. Which was maybe even weirder than the rest of it, that she would be so reliant for her emotional equilibrium on someone she hadn't even known a month ago.

He called on her cell that night, but she missed the call because she'd left her phone in her bag in her room while she visited with her new family.

By the time she realized he'd called, it was too late to call him back. It was one thing for him to initiate a phone call in the middle of the night his time and another thing for her to do so. Her mom had raised her to be courteous and she wouldn't wake him even if she wanted to talk to him so badly, it was an ache inside her.

She found it very difficult to get to sleep and called him first thing when she woke up. She hadn't even gotten out of bed, when she grabbed the bedside phone and dialed his number.

He answered on the second ring. "*Sí*, Miguel."

"Hi, Miguel." She smiled just saying his name. "It's Amber."

"Querida."

Her smile grew, the jumpy feelings inside her settling down at the sound of his voice. "I was really disappointed when I realized I'd missed your call last night."

"You were working?"

"Actually, I wasn't. I was talking with some people. I have so much to tell you."

"I too have news."

"You go first." She was fairly certain his wouldn't take as long and hers was confusing, even to herself.

She knew she wanted to tell him all about discovering she had a father and sister, but wasn't sure what words to use without making her mom sound bad. Which she wasn't. She was just a woman who loved really deeply.

"I will not be able to make the trip to California this week."

Her heart fell. She really needed to see him. "Oh."

"I am sorry, but perhaps it is for the best."

"For the best?"

"The more time we spend together, the more attached we become."

"That's a bad thing?" She rubbed her

temples. She was awake, right? Only this felt like a really disturbing dream.

"Considering the fact that I must go to Prague in five days and will be there an indefinite period of time, yes."

"But…"

"I know our association hasn't lasted as long as either of us would like."

Association? He was calling the incredible relationship developing between them an *association?* She needed him like the other half of her soul and he was talking like he didn't need her at all. Like the week in Spain had meant nothing.

"I don't…" Like both her sister and her mom—when faced with emotions too heavy to bear, she ran out of words.

He had plenty for both of them. "The truth, *querida?* I suspect it would take months to get my fill of you, but we did not have months and I am truly sorry about that."

He was sorry? Pain was coalescing inside her and *he was sorry?* She wanted to scream, but she forced out a question. "You don't want to try to maintain our relationship long distance?"

"It would not be fair to either of us."

He had not just said that. Finding out her

mom was not her biological mother, that she had a sister and father she hadn't known her whole life…those things were not fair. Getting her heart ripped out by the man she loved…that was not fair, but trying to make a long distance relationship work? What was so unfair about that? "Why not?"

He made a strange noise, but when he spoke his voice was even. "Your career is taking off. You will be very busy. Trying to work a long distance association would put an unnecessary strain on you."

"I'm willing." It hurt to say the words, pricked at her pride, but there were more important things than pride.

"It's too much, *querida,* surely you see that?"

No, she didn't, but then she didn't think it was all about her. Maybe not about her at all. "You said it wouldn't be fair to both of us."

"I am not keen on a cerebral relationship and that is all it could be for months, maybe longer."

"You mean you don't want to do without sex."

"Yes, but I do not think I am the only one this will be an issue for now. Now that your desires have awakened, they will not go back to sleep."

"You bastard."

He sucked in an audible breath. "Amber, we both went into our time together with open eyes."

"Apparently yours saw things mine didn't."

"You said yourself you were not ready for anything permanent."

Had she said that? Probably at one point. "Things change."

"I am sorry."

There was that sorry word again. She hated it. Her mom was sorry, too. She'd lied to Amber her whole life and she understood why, but it hurt to know the woman she trusted so implicitly could do that. Her dad was sorry he'd been such a rotten father to Ellie that Amber's mom had not felt safe making her known to him...to *them*.

None of the sorries changed anything. Didn't undo the pain of the past.

And then there was Miguel and his pathetic little sorry. She'd fallen in love with him and he thought he'd work her out of his system in months.

Sorry didn't make that okay.

She felt so stupid. All the things she thought meant she was special to him had been no more than the window dressing he'd given their affair. He'd even warned her, in the very beginning…his relationships were not based on emotion, but an exchange of commodities.

Not a cold exchange in their case when the commodity had been mutual passion, but still…not emotion…not love.

"Perhaps if we are both free of other entanglements when I return, we can connect again."

The words sliced through her already shattered emotions, cutting her heart loose from the fragile threads holding it to its moorings. He had no intention of avoiding other "entanglements"—that was obvious.

"So you can work me out of your system once and for all?" she asked in a voice like ground glass.

"As you said, things change. Given the right timing, who knows what could happen between us?"

"But now is not the right time."

"You know it is not."

She pulled the phone from her ear and stared at it. She knew the pain inside was from the words coming out of the phone, not the instrument, but she had this insane urge to pummel it with a hammer. Sounds were coming from the earpiece, but she couldn't make them out, didn't want to.

His words hurt her.

She pressed the end button and the sounds stopped.

But the pain didn't. Three days ago she had been happier than she'd ever been in her life, missing Miguel already, but happy. Now, everything was gone. Her hope for a future with him. Her belief in her life as she knew it.

The only thing that remained was her career and it was not the comfort it had always been. She wished she could be the mannequin she'd often compared herself to...no emotions, no pain lacerating her insides.

The phone chirped again a few minutes later, but she ignored it. When it rang a third time, she turned it off and threw it against the wall. It thumped and fell with an empty thud, nothing to satisfy the feelings raging through her.

A knock sounded on the door. "Amber, sweetheart, you need to be at your shoot in thirty minutes and I haven't heard the shower go."

Her mom's voice sounded hoarse, like she'd been crying. Amber could not afford to rage...to give into the pain...not right now.

Her mom needed her to be strong. She needed to be strong for herself. Using the techniques she'd taught herself to get centered for a shoot, she pulled the emotions in until they were contained deep inside.

Another knock sounded. "Amber…are you all right?"

"Fine." Her own lie added to all those her mom had told her…for the same good cause, though. Right? "I'll be out in a little bit."

"Okay, honey."

"Thanks, Mom." Was that normal voice hers?

How could it be? But she had to keep it together. There was too much emotional turmoil surrounding them already at the moment. She'd tell her mom about Miguel. Later. After her dad and sister had gone home to Boston. After she was sure her mom was going to be okay emotionally as well as legally.

Amber would be strong for her mom. Strong for herself, she couldn't rely on anyone else.

CHAPTER TEN

ONLY Amber didn't tell her. She didn't see the need. Her mom asked about Miguel once and Amber told her about his trip to Prague. Things *did* heat up with her career and she was so busy working, she saw her mom rarely.

When Helen told her that she was going to work for George Wentworth and moving to Boston so Amber could spend her off time getting to know her family there, she was relieved her mom would not be alone. She kept the house in California as a home base, though. She knew they all expected her to go to Boston, that her mom had moved to make it easier for her, but she couldn't do it. She needed time to come to terms with where her life had gone.

Her sister got married and Amber flew to Boston to be maid of honor. She spent the two days she had with her family wearing the smile that had launched her career. The nausea had started a couple of weeks after she and Miguel broke up, but she didn't worry about it. Stress could do that to a person.

She didn't feel much like eating anyway, so when she was nauseous, she didn't. She got a commercial spot and found it easy to lose the five pounds her agent wanted her to. She started wearing more makeup to hide the circles under her eyes from lack of sleep.

When she slept, she dreamed. About Miguel. They weren't nightmares, far from it…she relived every moment in his arms, but waking up hurt like someone was pounding her chest with an anvil. Easier not to sleep at all than to deal with the pain on waking.

She was driving to a shoot two hours from her home when the lack of sleep caught up with her. She woke in an area hospital. Her body ached, but not like anything was broken. Like she was having a really bad period.

She moaned and forced her eyes to open.

No one else was in the emergency cubicle.

"Miss Taylor?"

She looked up as the doctor came in. At least she assumed it was the doctor. "Yes?"

"How do you feel?"

"Not so good."

"It could be a lot worse."

"Yes."

"When you fell asleep, your foot relaxed on the accelerator and impact happened at less than thirty miles per hour we figure."

"Was anyone else hurt?" She couldn't stand the thought of being responsible for someone else's pain.

"No other cars were involved."

"I didn't break anything?"

"How do you feel?" he asked, instead of answering.

"Achy. Like I'm having a bad monthly."

"I'm sorry, Miss Taylor."

Something in his eyes said he meant more than commiseration for cramps. "What's wrong with me?"

"You lost the baby."

"Baby?" She'd been pregnant? But she and Miguel had been so careful.

"You didn't know you were pregnant?"

"No."

"That explains you not taking care of yourself."

She stared at him, the silent criticism screaming through her brain. She hadn't known she was carrying a baby. She hadn't taken care of the baby. Her baby was dead because she'd fallen asleep at the wheel.

When she lurched up in bed, the doctor seemed to know exactly what she needed and had the small elliptically shaped dish near her mouth before she was sick on the sheets of the pristine hospital bed. Pristine and white. No blood anywhere. Her baby was already gone.

She checked herself out of the hospital a few hours later after calling her agent and telling him a portion of the truth. She'd been in an accident. She didn't tell her mom anything, just went home and prepared for the next day's shoot.

The nausea did not leave with the end of her pregnancy. The thought of food sickened her. She had not eaten enough to keep her pregnancy viable, she could not force herself to imbibe fuel for her own sake now. She didn't deserve it. She forced herself to sleep, though, no matter how much waking might hurt.

She couldn't risk falling asleep at the wheel again and hurting someone else.

She answered her cell phone five days after losing the baby and heard Miguel's voice on the other end of the line. "Don't ever call me again," she said in a voice that sounded dead even to her own ears and then hung up.

Three weeks later, her agent called her into his office. He was practically vibrating with anger as he tossed a set of photos onto the desk in front of her.

"What the bloody hell is this, Amber?"

She looked down at the pictures and tried to understand what had him so angry. Her smile was there. She'd posed exactly as the photographer had asked her to. She looked back at her agent with a question in her eyes.

"You look like a flippin' skeleton."

"You told me to lose weight for the commercial."

"That was ten, maybe fifteen pounds... hell, honey, I can't tell how much weight you've lost, ago. You want to tell me why you're trying to kill yourself slowly?"

"I'm not."

"Then, explain this." He waved with anger at the pictures.

She shrugged. "Is the client mad?"

"Mad? I don't know. They refused to use the pictures and got another model for the gig. You tell me."

"Oh. Maybe we should concentrate on commercials then."

"You aren't a flippin' actress, Amber Taylor. You're a model and you're going to be a dead model if you don't start eating."

She didn't know what to say. She wasn't going to die. That was silly. So, she'd lost some weight. "I'll try to gain a few pounds back."

"Good."

But she couldn't make herself eat. She couldn't make herself feel. She understood how her father could have turned off all emotion. It was the only way to control the pain. She hoped that if she had a child, she would not abandon it, but she didn't. Her baby was dead and she could not stand to feel anymore.

She thought of her sister and how the other woman had kept loving in spite of a lifetime of rejection. How odd that Amber would turn out more like their father despite being raised by a loving mom than Ellie who had been raised in a dearth of emotion.

A week later, she walked into the house to find her sister, her mom, her dad and Sandor Christofides ensconced in the living room waiting for her.

Her sister gasped when she saw Amber. Her dad said a truly ugly word and Amber's mom started to cry. "Baby, I don't know what's happening, but you've got to let us help."

"Is this about Miguel?" Ellie asked, proving that the instincts of a twin went beyond being raised in the same home or even aware of one another's existence.

Suddenly it all hit her…the loss of love before it had been fully realized, the loss of her baby, so precious and unknown to her, the loss of trust in life as she knew it. Everything inside Amber coalesced into a kind of hurt that sent her crumpling to the floor, a keening wail filling the air around her. Some distant part of her mind said she should go to whoever was hurting so much they were making that noise, but she was too wounded to move.

The next two months weren't easy. She had to force herself to eat with the same regimented dedication she had once forced herself not to eat for the sake of her career. The days were difficult to get through, the nights longer so much so.

She had stopped dreaming.

Miguel called again. She didn't bother to say anything this time. She simply hung up.

She still didn't feel, but her skeletal thinness was slowly going away and she did her level best to project a smiling countenance when she was with her family. It was on the day that her agent called her with the first job in weeks that she realized she didn't want to be a model any longer.

She finally understood that it had always been more than her body when she had nothing more to give to the camera. She went to work for her father and moved into his mansion, which seemed to make those around her happier. And that was all that mattered anymore.

Miguel felt like hell.

He'd spent twenty hours of the last forty-eight traveling and hadn't slept in longer than that. The last six months had been the most dismal of his life. The project was going fine, but he missed Amber like an amputated limb. And she wanted nothing to do with him.

He'd made a monumental mistake breaking up with her over the phone...or rather breaking up with her at all. He'd been worried about being fair to her, about his own ability to remain faithful when they saw each other rarely. Well, the last concern had been put to rest with no further doubts.

For the first time in his adult life, he'd been completely celibate for six months. And not because of lack of opportunity. There were many beautiful, sophisticated, sexually available women in Prague. However, none of them had sea-blue eyes he could drown in, or the endearing habit of biting a perfectly formed lower lip, or the fascination with history that his precious *querida* had exhibited.

None of them touched his heart or sent his libido into orbit with a simple look.

He'd realized his mistake early, but fought his feelings, sure they were temporary. While he'd never missed a woman before, he was confident that what he'd been feeling was not love. So damn sure of himself that he'd ignored his own heart because his mind said that love and marriage would come later in life, and not to a career minded woman he would have to share with the rest of the world.

For a man who was so rarely caught wrong, he'd done a spectacular job of messing up.

He'd finally given into his urges to call her and she'd told him she never wanted to hear from him again and hung up on him. He'd tried to call back, but she hadn't answered. He'd been furious, or so he'd told himself for his pride's sake. It had taken another two months for him to acknowledge that what he felt was hurt and he'd tried calling again.

This time she had not even done him the courtesy of speaking. She'd simply hung up and it was then that he realized he was not dealing with an angry woman, but one who was in pain. And he felt like hell, knowing it was his fault. Maybe she was better off without a selfish bastard like himself in her life.

He'd convinced himself of that for another two months. Until the weekly report came in from his investigator. Okay, he was obsessed, but he needed her. She refused to have anything to do with him, so he kept track of her, got copies of all her work, watched the commercial she'd made over and over again until he felt like some kind of seedy stalker.

He thought she looked like something was missing…her spark of animation. Then he would tell himself he was being self-serving believing that. But when the report came back that she was no longer modeling and had canceled her contract with her agent, he knew something was very wrong and he was determined to find out what and fix it.

If he could.

He tormented himself with the thought that she might have found someone else, but the investigator had no evidence of her dating. Not that he was watching her that closely. Miguel wasn't really a stalker. Nor was he willing to invade her privacy completely. But there was no public evidence that Amber had gotten involved with another man.

Grateful for that small favor, Miguel stumbled into the hotel room in California. He would sleep and then go to see Amber tomorrow.

His cell rang and he thought about letting it go, but saw the caller was his investigator.

He flipped the phone open. "Menendez here."

The investigator spoke in rapid Catalan, but Miguel had no trouble understanding.

"Amber is living with her mother in George Wentworth's home? And she's working for him? In what capacity?"

He didn't know what shocked him the most, that Amber had moved away from her beloved warm beach, that she was living with a man old enough to be her father or that she was working for him. But the investigators next revelation, sent Miguel's mind reeling in a free fall.

George Wentworth's daughter was almost a mirror image of Amber Taylor. The investigator had done some further checking and discovered that Wentworth had twin daughters, but one of them had disappeared from the hospital less than a week after birth. There was only one conclusion to draw from this, considering how alike Amber and Eleanor Christofides were in looks. Amber was George Wentworth's daughter.

Miguel didn't know how her mom fit into this strange turn of events, but the fact that she was living in Wentworth's house right now, too, said something.

He was tempted to order an immediate flight to the East Coast, but common sense prevailed. If he was exhausted, his pilot would be, too. He needed sleep before seeing Amber and time to digest this new information.

He called and ordered an early morning takeoff instead, then despite all the stuff crowding his brain, he slept.

* * *

Amber schooled her features into a pleasant expression and then went downstairs to meet her family for dinner. Ellie and Sandor were here, too, and she knew that she had to be careful to project positive emotion or her sister was going to start asking questions again.

In some dim part of her brain, it surprised her that her mom was easier to fool than her sister. But maybe that was because Helen Taylor seemed as intrigued by George Wentworth as Amber was. Though for obviously different reasons.

At first, Amber had thought the interest *was* because he was her father, but after moving to Boston, she'd come to see that her mom's fascination with her father was much more personal. She was glad for her mom even if the joy didn't reach all the way inside. Her brain told her this was a good thing and that if her heart could feel anything, it would be happy.

Ellie was smiling and chatting with their father when Amber walked into the living room, but her sister jumped up and rushed over for a hug when she saw her.

Amber returned the embrace, careful not to pull away too quickly.

Ellie kept hold of her arms as she stepped

back a little and looked to Amber closely. "You look great."

"Thank you. You, too." Ellie didn't dress as trendily as Amber, but she always looked nice and this evening was no exception.

"How are you liking your new job?"

"I like it, more than I expected even, but Mom's fascination with financial details rubbed off somewhere along the way."

"And she's wonderful at it, too," her mom chimed in, her voice warm.

"So her supervisor tells me," her dad said with a smile and a small one-armed hug for her mom.

Weird. This thing between them was strange. Good, but definitely strange. She now realized that her mom's inability to fall for another guy had as much to do with her fear of what would happen when Amber was discovered for who she really was as her great love for Len Taylor.

"It is all good," Sandor added, completing the round of approval for her new job.

She'd been a little stunned at first that no one had demurred when she'd said she didn't want to be a model anymore. Then she'd latched onto the fact from a couple of things her mom and sister had said that they blamed her career in part for her near death experience from self-enforced starvation.

They blamed Miguel, too, and the stress of learning she'd been kidnapped as a baby. Her mom still felt guilty, no matter what Amber said. She hated that, but she couldn't admit the truth. That her inability to eat was her own fault...she was the one who had killed her baby.

She couldn't admit that to them, though.

If she allowed herself to feel, the grief and guilt would overwhelm her.

Ellie was looking at her worriedly again and she realized she'd let her façade of contentment slip. She was pulling it back into place, trying to project warm friendliness in her eyes when the doorbell rang. Seconds later her dad's housekeeper led Miguel Menendez into the room.

He looked haggard. Dark circles under his eyes, thinner than she'd last seen him and his complexion was almost sallow with stress and fatigue. Even so, he was the most gorgeous thing her eyes had ever set on.

Shouldn't she hate the sight of him? But

she didn't…only the feelings trying to break through her self-imposed barrier.

He ignored everyone else in the room and focused entirely on her. "*Querida,* we need to talk."

The world went dark around the edges. She swayed.

He lurched toward her, his arms stretched out and he swore. In Chinese. Like the first time he cursed around her.

For some reason that was more than she could take and the blackness descended like a welcome blanket.

When she opened her eyes, he was there.

"Go away."

"No."

She glared, a surge of anger going through her. "I don't want to see you."

"Yes, you do. I screwed up. I need to fix it. We need each other."

She sat up and realized she was on her bed. On top of the covers, not beneath them. "I don't need you. Go away!"

A gasp from beside her had her head swerving. Her sister was next to her on the bed; Sandor stood beside her, his hand on her shoulder. Her mom stood just behind Miguel, looking as shocked as Amber felt. Like the first time she'd seen him, her dad was comforting her mom. It was sweet, but she wished they'd all go away. Not just Miguel.

All of them.

She didn't need Miguel. She didn't. She didn't want to need anyone. She didn't deserve to. She hadn't been there for the tiny being who had needed her and no one else. She'd let that newly formed person down.

Pain clogged her throat and she realized she was swallowing back tears. This wasn't right. She couldn't feel. She didn't want to.

"Go away, Miguel, please—" Her voice broke and she had to breathe deeply to keep the tears at bay.

"I am not going anywhere."

"That is not for you to say. This is my home and I'll be damned if I'll let you stay here and upset my daughter."

Miguel didn't look shocked at that revealing speech. He didn't look impacted by it at all. His eyes never left her face. "You are mine, Amber, and I am yours."

"No." She shook her head, frantic for him to leave. "I can't be yours. Not anymore."

"That's it." Her dad's hand landed on

Miguel's shoulder and her Catalan ex-lover tensed as if ready for battle.

"Stop it." That was Ellie's voice, as sharp as a drill sergeant's and shocking everyone in the room. "Knock it off, Dad."

Amber wanted to look at her sister, ask her what she thought she was doing, but she couldn't drag her gaze away from Miguel.

"Don't tell me you've decided to champion this man's case, Ellie. You know how much he hurt your sister."

"I know he looks as bad as she does when she thinks no one is watching. I know I saw the same grief and wild despair in his eyes when she fainted I saw in hers that day we went to get her in California. I know that for the first time in months my sister's voice is ringing with real emotion, even if it's anger. It's real."

"She was getting better..." That was her mom, but Amber couldn't make herself look at her, either.

Miguel's gray eyes were eating her alive and she felt them on her skin, like she'd felt nothing else since she woke up in the hospital and learned she'd lost the baby she hadn't even known about.

"No, she wasn't getting better, she was getting more proficient at hiding her lack of feeling. She loves us all enough to pretend, but it has been just that…a pretense. I tried to convince myself it wasn't, but seeing her when Miguel came into the living room, I know it was. You all know it was."

The sound of fabric sliding against fabric and her mom's voice came as if muffled by a large male chest. "She's right. God in Heaven help us…but she's right."

There were tears in her mom's voice and Amber wanted to comfort her, but she couldn't move.

"I don't know what happened between you and my sister, Mr. Menendez, but I think you might be the only person who can bring her back from the place she's been living for months."

"No." The word whispered out of Amber's mouth before she knew it was there.

Ellie's hand grasped hers. "Yes, baby. I know he hurt you, but he's hurting, too. There has to be a way back for both of you."

Finally…finally…Amber looked away from Miguel to her sister. "There isn't. It's gone."

"Your heart isn't gone anymore than Dad's

was after Mom died, but I'll be darned if I'm going to spend the next two decades waiting for you to come back to us like I waited on him. Near death woke him up, but you would have died from not eating, too. The doctors said your organs were dangerously close to shutting down, but it didn't matter. You still didn't come back."

"I started eating again."

"But you still don't want to feel. You aren't living. You're just existing."

"I am living. For all of you."

Tears spilled over Ellie's eyes. "Amber, baby, we need you to live for you. We all love you so much."

"I can't stand to be around Miguel."

"Please, Amber...just talk to him. If you want Dad and Sandor to throw him out afterward, then they will...but please, do this... for me."

"But why?"

"Because I think he can help you heal."

"He can't give me back what I lost."

"No, but maybe he can give you something else instead. Maybe not. Maybe you really do hate him, but, honey, you are real for the first time in weeks...months even. I need you to talk to him, to keep the realness going. If only to tell him he's a selfish bastard who doesn't deserve you."

"I already know that." Miguel's voice was rocky and the words were too much for Amber's fragile hold on her emotions.

She turned wild eyes to him. "It's not like that. Please, I…" Her throat closed and she had to concentrate to get more words out. "Privacy…" She gulped in air, wondering why it was so hard to breathe. "If we're going to talk…we need privacy."

CHAPTER ELEVEN

ELLIE squeezed her hand and then stood. "Come on, everyone."

"Amber," her mom said in a pleading voice and she forced herself to look at her. "Sweetheart, I can't lose you…not like this. You've got to be okay."

Amber nodded. "I know."

"Will you eat before you talk?"

Her roiling stomach made her want to refuse, but she knew how important this was to her mom, how important it was to *her* if she wanted to stay healthy.

"Maybe a tray?"

"I'll bring one up."

"Bring food for Miguel, too."

"I am not hungry."

She turned fierce eyes on him. "If I have to eat, so do you. You look like you've lost a stone and you didn't have a stone to lose."

There was satisfaction in being the one doing the haranguing in this area.

Her dad actually laughed. It was such a nice sound and Amber realized one that had been all too infrequent over the past months. "Listen to her, son."

"*Anything*." Miguel's face twisted with emotion. "If it will make you happy."

Amber stared. Would it make her happy if he ate? She didn't think so, but...but... "I would be satisfied."

"Then I will eat."

They waited in silence, neither making the slightest effort to break it or move from their positions on her bed, until her mom returned with a tray laden with two dinner plates and juice to drink. "Eat first, talk after," she admonished and then left.

And that is what Miguel and Amber did. They ate.

When they were finished, Miguel took the tray and put it on the floor. Then he turned back to face her, his expression as ravaged as her sister had alluded to. "Your sister said you almost died...from not eating?"

She nodded.

He swallowed, his eyes glistening in a way

she couldn't accept as real. "Why?" he asked in a whisper.

Terror coursed through her. No one else had asked that. They'd all assumed they knew the answer and she'd let them go on believing it. So, she hadn't had to lie. Could she lie to him? Could she pretend that it was what everyone else believed it had been?

But he was the baby's father. He deserved to know. Didn't he? He'd rejected her, but that didn't mean he didn't have the right to know. But she hadn't admitted her culpability to anyone. Not even the E.R. doctor, though she was sure he suspected.

Miguel waited without speaking, apparently willing to sit like that all night while she worked through the thoughts swirling in her head. Oh, but his eyes spoke and the message in them was so filled with emotion she wanted to hide.

He was feeling enough for both of them and she didn't understand how that could be. He was the one who had not wanted to try to have a long distance relationship, but he looked like a man who had been abandoned by love. Not vice versa.

She licked her lips. "A couple of weeks

after I got back from Spain, I got nauseous. It was an all day thing and my agent wanted me to lose a few pounds for a commercial."

"You did not have a few pounds to lose."

She shrugged. "It was easy to stop eating at all when food made me feel sick. I wasn't sleeping, either. The dreams…they got to me and I hated waking up to loneliness."

"I am sorry." He made a pained sound, his hands fisting against his thighs with white knuckle intensity.

"Miguel?"

He shook his head, like he was trying to pull himself together. "You almost died. I could not have stood that and I know it is my fault."

He sounded like that knowledge was killing him. And it wasn't true. "No. I worked out that you'd never once lied to me or led me on. I just assumed that if it was so special for me, it must be for you, too."

"It was special."

She could have argued, but it didn't matter anymore. That part of her life was gone. She didn't know if he wanted to sleep with her again, or to be her friend, or what, but she didn't want any of it. She'd talk to him because Ellie was right…she needed to, but then he was leaving and she didn't want to see him again.

"Anyway, I didn't take care of myself. Not your fault. Mine. I should have, but I didn't. I fell asleep at the wheel while driving to a shoot. I woke up in Emergency and my baby was gone."

"Your baby?" he asked in a faint voice, surging up from the bed and falling almost immediately back to sit on it—as if his legs would not hold him. "You were pregnant?" he croaked.

Should she have softened the blow some way? Probably, only she didn't know how. What else could she say? "Yes. And we were so careful, I don't know how it happened, but it did and I didn't protect my baby and I'll never forgive myself," she admitted the deepest pain of her heart.

"The first time…we were not so careful." He was gray beneath the dusky tone of his skin. "Our baby…is dead." This time, the shimmer in his eyes was obvious moisture and a tear slid down that he seemed totally unaware of. "You almost died. I did not protect either of you," he grated in a voice like sandpaper.

"It wasn't your job." It had been hers and she had messed up. Horribly.

"So…after the…" He paused, swallowed and made a visible effort to pull himself together. "After the baby, you stopped eating altogether?"

"I starved our baby…I deserved to starve myself."

"No!" He grabbed her shoulders, his expression like the damned. "No, Amber. Do not say this…do not think this…not ever again!"

"I can't help thinking it." Truth was like that. It wouldn't leave you alone.

"You must. It is wrong. So very wrong. You lost the baby after the accident, no?"

"Yes."

"If you had starved the baby, you would have lost it before that…the baby depleted your strength when you had none to give. You gave the last of yourself to the baby and nearly killed yourself in the process." Another tear slid down his cheek and he swiped at with impatience this time, as if annoyed with his own weakness.

"I killed our baby."

Miguel thought he might be sick. He had thought he had hurt before, but the pain of missing her was nothing like this. To know that she had almost died...that their baby was dead. It was worse than anything he could imagine...except maybe if she had died. And for her to believe it was her fault when he had been the one to let her down.

Every word was a slashing knife wound in his heart. He did not know the words to convince her otherwise, but he had to try. "You might as well say I killed her, because you would not have been so distraught if I had not rejected our love."

He wished he could believe she thought that, even a little. She should, but it was so clear she was taking all the blame on herself and he could not stand it.

"We never said we loved each other."

"But it was there all the same, was it not?"

She shook her head.

But he knew she lied. She had loved and so had he even if he had been too stupid to see it until too late. However, he was not going to push that particular issue right now.

This was more important. "You are not responsible for the death of our baby."

"Yes, I am. If I had been taking proper care of myself—"

"Which you would have been if I had not hurt you, if you had realized you were pregnant, but you did not."

"I should have."

"No, why would you? You had never even had sex before me…you had no experience with these things. You had every reason to believe the nausea was a result of stress. You'd learned your father was not who you believed him to be, your life was changed irrevocably…I had let you down when you needed me most." Would he ever forgive himself for that? He did not know, but he would do his best to spend a lifetime not repeating that mistake. "Your stress level was phenomenal. I should have recognized love when it smacked me in the face, but I did not and you and our baby paid the price."

He shuddered inside with the knowledge of how close he'd come to losing them both.

"No…I… You don't love me, Miguel."

"I do."

She shook her head and he almost smiled. But he was hurting too much for even dark humor to get through. Only if he had ever considered a woman's reaction to him saying he loved her, it would not have been denial. But maybe with this woman and the way he'd treated her, it was the only reaction that made sense.

He could not change the past, only work on their future. And they did have a future. Together. Because apart, they were both only partial people.

"I don't want to talk anymore."

"You need to rest, but I do not want to leave you."

"You have to leave."

He was not so sure about that, but he said nothing. He would talk to her father after he left her to rest.

He leaned down and pressed a chaste kiss to her soft lips. "We will talk more tomorrow."

"No."

"Sleep," he said instead of answering.

There was no point in arguing something he was determined to win.

When he went downstairs, they were all waiting for him in the living room.

Ellie, the sister, was looking expectant. Her husband faintly menacing and her father much the same. Helen Taylor looked like she was terrified to hear what he had to say and just as frightened of leaving it unsaid.

"I would like to stay here, if I may," he

said, coming straight to the point. It felt like begging, but he had to stay near her. He and Amber had too much to work through. And after learning he had almost lost her to starvation, he could not make himself leave her…even to find a hotel.

"Did she talk to you?" Ellie asked when her father didn't answer Miguel's request right away.

"Yes, her guilt over the baby is immense, but I'm determined to help her work through it and come to see that she is not at fault."

"Baby?" her mother asked in a voice similar to the one he'd used upon hearing.

And it was only then that he realized none of these people had known. Damn it, if he'd been thinking straight, he would have wondered…been circumspect until he could ask her. However, even knowing how devastated she had been, he was stunned to realize she hadn't shared something so shattering with her beloved mother.

The words could not be unsaid however. The only choice was to move forward. "I think perhaps there is a great deal we need to tell each other."

* * *

Amber woke to her alarm the next morning having slept fourteen hours straight. She had forced herself to sleep since the accident, but had not rested so well since returning from Spain.

She showered in her en suite and dressed in a faux suede pantsuit in alligator print by Tesori. It was only a little loose, which filled her with satisfaction. She was getting better physically. That was good for her family.

Maybe even for her.

She wasn't completely shocked to see Miguel at the breakfast table, though the way he and her father were chatting like old friends took her aback. *That* she had not expected.

Both men looked up on her entrance and smiled.

Her dad's expression mirrored a lack of tension she only now realized had been there because it was gone. "Good morning, Amber. You look like you slept well."

"I did." She returned his smile.

"That is good to hear," Miguel said, his expression a little more difficult to read than her father's.

"Where's Mom?" she asked as she sat down

and waited for the housekeeper to bring her breakfast.

"Right here," said a feminine voice from the doorway.

She came over and hugged Amber before kissing George's cheek and then sitting down. She nodded at Miguel. "Good morning, Miguel. I trust you slept well."

He gave a noncommittal shrug. "I hope to spend the morning with Amber. Will that be a problem?"

"Why are you asking her?" Amber inquired, feeling genuinely confused. Miguel might be arrogant, but he wasn't the type to treat her like her opinion didn't matter.

"I learned last night that she was your direct supervisor. I do not want to interrupt your work schedule, but I do want to talk."

"Oh." Brilliant. As conversational gambits went, that was stellar. *Not*. But she wasn't sure what *to* say.

She'd been adamant the night before that she didn't want to see him anymore, but in the light of morning, she realized he was giving her an opportunity to have closure on a painful part of her life and she should take it.

"There's no problem on my end with

Amber taking the morning off," her mom said, a quaver in her voice Amber didn't understand.

She turned to look her mom full in the face and saw grief in the blue eyes that she did not understand. "What's the matter?"

"I don't understand why you didn't tell me. Or maybe I do. I suppose you decided you couldn't trust me after finding out what I did. I..." Tears filled her eyes and she shook her head. "I'm sorry, I promised myself I wouldn't do this."

It clicked in Amber's brain and she turned to Miguel. "You told them?"

"I did not realize you had not. I am very sorry, *querida*. I would not have done so had I known, but I was unaware things had changed so drastically between you and your mother."

"They didn't." Amber felt like things were cracking open inside her and she was scared to deal with them, but from the pain-filled expression in her mother's drenched eyes, she knew she had to.

She jumped up and hugged her mom tight. "They didn't, Mom. Believe me. I just...I was so ashamed of what I'd done. I couldn't tell anyone. Not even you."

"But you didn't do anything."

"I killed my baby."

Miguel made a hoarse sound of protest, but it was her father's foul curse that caught her attention. He was on his feet and coming around the table to put his arms around both her and her mom. "You didn't kill your baby, Amber. The accident happened and you have to learn to live with it, but it's called an accident because it wasn't deliberate."

Amber shook her head.

"Honey, I understand guilt, but you've got to let it go. I almost lost both you and your sister because of mine. I should have been driving the night your mother died. But I was working and she went to dinner with friends without me. I should have been protecting you and Ellie in the nursery, but I was too busy grieving to be there when Helen took you. I could have saved her, you...all of us so much pain. But I have to move on from that knowledge. We all do."

"But, Daddy...I stopped eating. I fell asleep because I wasn't sleeping at night, trying to hide from my pain."

"Baby, you didn't do anything wrong. You

were trying to cope and it was too much. We'll all miss the baby, but losing you, too, like we have for the past few months…that's even worse. We all need you. And you needed us and none of us realized it until it was almost too late. We could apportion blame from now to eternity, but the only way to heal is to let it go. Let the guilt go and let us help you deal with the pain."

The words were so healing, but she was still scared. "Mom?" Amber asked, afraid of what her mom would think of her now that she knew the truth.

But Helen Taylor looked at her with wisdom born of her own experience. "Sweetheart, if anyone understands guilt and pain, it's me. We do the best we can and sometimes it just isn't enough. If you'd realized you were pregnant, you would never have done anything to put your baby at risk."

"But it's gone…"

"I know, baby, I know."

And then all three of them were crying together and Miguel was there on the outer edges. His granitelike presence giving her comfort. Why that should be, she did not know, but it did. And then he was there, pushing into the midst of them, pulling her against him and she melted into his embrace as if he was her rock. With her parents' arms around them both, they cried together for the loss of their baby.

When the tears had finally abated, her mom and dad were no longer holding her and Miguel, but were sitting together, watching them with matching expressions of hope on their faces. She didn't know what they hoped for, but she could guess.

Why didn't anyone understand that it was over between her and Miguel? Maybe because in expressing her deepest pain she had clung most strongly to him, her mind whispered. She ignored the small voice and allowed Miguel to mop her face while she tried to collect the emotions spilling like an overflowing river all around her.

Emotions she had genuinely believed were gone.

He kissed her forehead and it felt like a benediction. "We need to talk."

"Yes." There was more to say, though she wasn't exactly sure what. It just felt like things were not quite finished between them.

"First we eat."

"Both of us," she said with a small smile.

He nodded, his lips not quite curving, but his eyes filled with warmth.

Her mom and dad showed a tremendous amount of tact by actually going into the office and leaving Amber and Miguel alone but for the servants and security detail in the house.

Even so, she decided she wanted to go back to her bedroom where they could talk without any interruption.

They sat in the matching armchairs that faced the small fireplace at one end of her large room.

He caught her gaze and held it, determination burning in his eyes along with a lingering pain that caught at something she thought was dead in her heart. "I love you, Amber. I want to be with you."

She hadn't been expecting that. She really hadn't. Wasn't sure why not, after all, he'd made the claim the day before. But somehow, she had expected he'd want to talk about the baby, their breakup, anything but his supposed love for her.

She shook her head. "You can't."

"I do."

She spoke the only truth that mattered

any longer. "You don't belong to me any-more, Miguel."

"You are wrong. I am yours as you are mine."

"No." She shook her head, but wasn't able to look away from him any more than she'd been able to the night before.

"Yes. I have been yours from that after-noon in Spain when we made love for the first time. Despite my stupidity on the phone, I have not touched another woman since you. Had no desire to do so. In my heart we were always together."

She almost choked on her shock. Miguel was an alpha male to his toes…talking about love and hearts was…well, it had to be as foreign to him as Chinese was for her.

But she steeled herself against that knowl-edge and said, "Well, in mine, we weren't. You broke up with me because you didn't think I was worth trying to be celibate for— or making a commitment to—and I lived with knowledge. And when our baby died… when I almost died…you were nowhere around. If you had been mine, you would have been there. Stop deluding yourself, Miguel. I don't know why you're so intent on renewing a relationship that should never have happened, but it's got nothing to do with undying love."

"You are so sure of that?"

"Absolutely."

"And yet, I do love you."

"Your brand of love is deadly, Miguel. I don't want it."

"But you admit it is love?"

"No, only what you call love is bad for me." And she finally recognized the metallic taste in her mouth. It was fear. Absolute terror in fact. She couldn't let him in again because doing so the first time had almost destroyed her. This time, she might not survive. She almost hadn't the first time.

Maybe it was irrational, but she associated him as deeply with their baby's death as she did herself and with her own near death. She hadn't realized it until now, but that terror was undeniable. Loving Miguel was deadly.

"There's nothing to salvage between us."

"I think there is and I will convince you."

She shook her head.

"I once showed you Barcelona, will you return the favor for me now?"

"If I do, will you go away?" she asked desperately.

"I can't." At least he didn't lie. "I need you and I believe you need me. I will prove to you that you can trust me again." He looked consideringly at her. "Your sister thinks it is a good idea."

"My sister believes in fairy tales, but then she's living out her happy ending."

"Perhaps I can convince you to believe again, too."

She got up and went to her bureau drawer and grabbed a packet of pictures. She tossed them at him.

He opened them, his breath hissing out and curses in several languages filling the stillness of the room.

"You know it doesn't do any good to swear in Chinese if I can figure out what you're saying from your tone of voice."

"But you don't know the words I'm using and they aren't something I would ever repeat in your company." His jaw clenched, though, as he obviously bit back more angry epitaphs while he went through the pictures. Pain sliced through him.

She wished he'd just go ahead and swear. He was vibrating with anger. She wasn't sure why, though. The pictures were a stack her agent had sent to her family when she'd gotten so far underweight. They showed her progression from too thin to dangerously starved. They were the reason her family had been waiting for her in the house in California that fateful day.

"Loving you is dangerous for me."

"Only when I did not recognize my love for you."

"I almost died, Miguel. Our baby did die."

"And you blame me as much as you blame yourself…perhaps more."

"No. Maybe. I don't know. I just know that I don't want to love you."

"You do not have a choice." His hands gripped the armrests tightly, like he wanted to touch her but had to hold back. "I'm more sorry than I can say that I hurt you, *querida,* but if I have learned one thing in the last six months, it is that love does not come to order. And finally, I am grateful for it because I cannot live happily without you. We will find our way together again."

"We won't."

"We will. Give me time…show me your new home, share your days with me. Give us a chance."

"I'm scared."

"So, am I."

She stared at him.

He shook his head, still red rimmed eyes boring into her. "Do you think after seeing those photos I am not terrified right out of my arrogance?"

"I don't understand."

"Tell me what you would feel if I walked in front of a bus and you came to the hospital to find me on the verge of death."

Her heart stopped. "Don't say things like!"

"Exactly. Those pictures scare the hell out of me because they show me how fragile your life was, how fragile it could be again. I will not let that ever happen again."

"Only I can stop it."

"I will help you."

She wanted to believe him and the desire shocked her spitless. She wanted to trust him? "I'll show you around Boston…a little."

He smiled at the caveat.

"No sex."

His eyes filled with pain. "Understood."

She stood firm that first day, and the next, and the one after that, but he remained…a permanent fixture it felt like…in her father's home. Miguel was there for breakfast; he was there at the office offering to take her to lunch; he was there when she came home. He shared their family dinners and treated her parents with a friendliness that belied any early animosity between them.

And it felt frighteningly right.

She kept her promise and showed him Boston…or at least a little of it. Their easy camaraderie returned when they played tourist and she looked forward to those times because they didn't force her to think too hard. Not like when he told her that he loved her…which he did two or three times a day. Each time, it touched something inside she didn't want touched. Made her feel things she thought she would never experience again.

On the fourth evening, her father took her mom out to dinner and the theater. That relationship was definitely moving forward and while Amber still found it almost mind-blowingly strange that those two should make a couple of it, she was very happy for them.

She and Miguel were in the living room after dinner, talking like they did in Spain, about everything.

Suddenly she just blurted out, "How long are you staying?"

"Forever, if that is what it takes."

"You've got to be kidding."

"I do?" He looked at her quizzically, his sexy gray eyes yet again touching those feelings she'd thought were dead.

And she found herself arguing more from habit than feeling. "You can't leave your job behind…what about your responsibilities to your company?"

He looked at her for several seconds of silence and then sighed. "Have you considered that if you had not discovered something about yourself that turned your life upside down, if you had…" He paused, took a deep breath, let it out…and went on. "Had you not lost our baby…my breaking off our relationship would not loom so largely as the insurmountable obstacle you perceive it to be?"

"Are you saying it wouldn't have hurt so much?" Because she doubted that. She'd loved him and he'd dismissed her as nothing in his life. Only, part of what he said resonated deep inside her.

Their relationship happened so fast, maybe

too fast for a man of his temperament to get his mind around it. She'd thought at first that since *she* could and she'd never even had a semirelationship, he should have been able to as well, but they were two different people. Yes…she could admit this inside her own head at least—they were basically compatible personalities, but different nonetheless.

He shook his head with a decisive jerk. "No, but I think you *would* have forgiven me…would have talked to me the first time I called. I could have groveled and we would have worked it out then instead of spending more months apart."

"You would not have groveled."

"Isn't that what I've been doing?"

"I…no…I…maybe. Gosh…sort of." And that made her feel better than she had in a long time, which didn't say much for her compassion and forgiveness level, did it? "But if that scenario had played out like you suggest, I would still be pursuing my modeling and a relationship between us *still* would not have worked according to you."

"You forget, I thought you *were* pursuing your career both the first and second time I called. I was willing…am willing to make whatever sacrifices are necessary to make the relationship work."

"You don't mean that." He couldn't. If he did, that would mean he really *did* love her…even after finding out about the baby… after everything.

"I am more serious than I have ever been." And his voice and expression testified to that truth. "You asked me how long I plan to stay…the answer is forever—if that is what it takes to make our relationship viable."

"No. You wouldn't do that. You're too dedicated to your family's company."

"I was…now, I have changed. Pain does that to a man. Speak to my father who will tell you that I was making plans to alter my responsibilities with Menendez Industries so that I could live near you in the States."

"Pain?"

"What do you think?" He rolled his eyes like she'd lost her mind and maybe she didn't blame him. "I missed you. I hurt you when I broke off our relationship, when I foolishly questioned my own ability to be faithful, but *I* hurt, too."

If he'd really cared…and she thought he had, of course he had hurt. She'd seen his pain over losing the baby. Over almost losing her. What had he said? Seeing the pictures of her too thin body had been like watching her walk in front of a bus. Hope welled deep inside, healing some pain, only comforting other.

She would always grieve the loss of her baby, but did she have to give up Miguel to make it all right? Nothing could make it okay, but choosing to love, to live in hope would make a difference, would make her own life of more value and maybe give her some kind of comfort for the tiny life that had been lost.

Miguel was looking at her with love burning in his eyes. Love she could choose to dismiss...or recognize. "I missed you even when I was telling you it was over between us. I have never regretted anything in my life as much as I regretted letting you believe I was putting you out of my life."

Hiding from her feelings had only brought more pain, dangerous consequences she never wanted to revisit. "But you never really let me go...in your heart." That's what he'd claimed and she finally believed him.

"Never. I could not and cannot let you go. Ever."

"Even after the baby?"

"I will grieve its loss for my entire life."

His words so like her own thoughts, made her eyes burn with healing tears.

He swallowed, as if trying to control his own emotions. "But if I lose you as well, I will never have another child."

She believed him. She had no choice, because she knew it was the same for her. If not Miguel...then no one. She'd known that since practically the first and that's why his breaking off with her had hurt so much. She knew she wouldn't just go on to another relationship, but he hadn't been able to, either, and he had not even realized then that he loved her.

She thought of the tiny life gone too soon and thought she could offer the tribute of forgiveness, both to herself and to Miguel to her baby's memory. She would never unwittingly hurt another because she was hiding from love, or the consequences of it.

"I've always wanted to go to Eastern Europe," she said quietly, emotions choking her and yet filling her with a joy she had not expected to feel again. Not ever.

He stared. "What?"

"But if I get pregnant again..." She stopped, savoring how right the words felt. And that surprised her, but she would not reject the gift of them, either. "I want to have my baby here...with my mom and my sister close."

He was out of the chair so fast, she barely saw him move and then he was leaning at her feet, his hands clasping hers. "You will marry me? You love me?"

"Yes."

"Say it."

"I will marry you."

His hands tightened on hers almost painfully. "And the other."

"I love you. I have since the afternoon we made love."

He groaned and took her mouth in a searing kiss. Minutes...hours...maybe even only seconds later, he lifted his head and smiled with a happiness that pierced her heart. "I love you."

"Always."

"Completely."

"Without limits."

"In every circumstance."

"Whatever life has to offer."

"You will have my love."

"And you will have mine."

They sealed their vows with a kiss as beautiful as a sunrise over the ocean.

EPILOGUE

AMBER looked out over the yacht rail. Miguel had insisted on taking her on a cruise to celebrate their second anniversary. They'd brought along the nanny for their twin boys. At her request, they'd also brought along her father and mother, now married. Ellie and Sandor and their little daughter. As well as Miguel's mother and father.

When he groaned about the lack of privacy, she reminded him that the other guests more than made up for it in baby-sitting so they could have quiet time as a couple.

Amber had lived the first twenty-four years of her life with her mom as her only family, but now she was surrounded by people she loved and who loved her, but none more than the amazing and truly wonderful man she'd married.

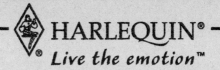

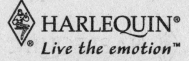

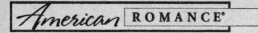
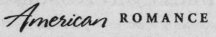
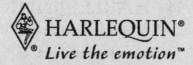

HARLEQUIN®
INTRIGUE®

BREATHTAKING ROMANTIC SUSPENSE

Shared dangers and passions lead to electrifying
romance and heart-stopping suspense!

Every month, you'll meet six new heroes
who are guaranteed to make your spine tingle
and your pulse pound. With them you'll enter
into the exciting world of Harlequin Intrigue—
where your life is on the line
and so is your heart!

THAT'S INTRIGUE—
ROMANTIC SUSPENSE
AT ITS BEST!

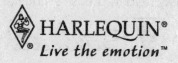

HARLEQUIN®
Live the emotion™

passionate powerful provocative love stories

Silhouette® Desire

**Silhouette Desire delivers
strong heroes, spirited heroines
and compelling love stories.**

Desire features your favorite authors,
including

Annette Broadrick,
Diana Palmer,
Maureen Child
and Brenda Jackson.

**Passionate, powerful and provocative
romances *guaranteed!***

For superlative authors, sensual stories
and sexy heroes, choose Silhouette Desire.

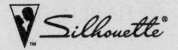

passionate powerful provocative love stories